Strange Men Strange Places

Ruskin Bond has been writing for over sixty years, and has now over 120 titles in printnovels, collections of stories, poetry, essays, anthologies and books for children. His first novel, *The Room on the Roof*, received the prestigious John Llewellyn Rhys award in 1957. He has also received the Padma Shri (1999), the Padma Bhushan (2014) and two awards from the Sahitya Akademione for his short stories and another for his writings for children. In 2012, the Delhi government gave him its Lifetime Achievement Award.

Born in 1934, Ruskin Bond grew up in Jamnagar, Shimla, New Delhi and Dehradun. Apart from three years in the UK. he has spent all his life in India, and now lives in Mussoorie with his adopted family.

A shy person, Ruskin says he likes being a writer because When Im writing theres nobody watching me. Today, its hard to find a profession where youre not being watched!

Strange Men Strange Places

Ruskin Bond

RUPA

Published by
Rupa Publications India Pvt. Ltd 1992
7/16, Ansari Road, Daryaganj
New Delhi 110002

Sales centres:
Bengaluru Chennai
Hyderabad Jaipur Kathmandu
Kolkata Mumbai Prayagraj

Copyright © Ruskin Bond 1992

All rights reserved.
No part of this publication may be reproduced, transmitted, or stored
in a retrieval system, in any form or by any means, electronic,
mechanical, photocopying, recording or otherwise,
without the prior permission of the publisher.

P-ISBN: 978-81-716-7107-6
E-ISBN: 978-81-291-2848-5

Twelfth impression 2023

15 14 13 12

The moral right of the author has been asserted.

Typeset by Mindways Design

Printed in India

This book is sold subject to the condition that it shall not, by way of trade
or otherwise, be lent, resold, hired out, or otherwise circulated, without
the publisher's prior consent, in any form of binding or cover other than
that in which it is published.

To the memory of my father
who, when I was a small boy, led me by the
hand up the steps of old forts and palaces,
these memorials of forgotten
men and places

ACKNOWLEDGEMENT

The chapters on Gardner, Skinner and de Boigne first appeared as articles the author wrote for *The Illustrated Weekly of India*. Most of the material in the other chapters has been used by him in articles for *The Hindu, The Hindustan Times, Hindusthan Standard, The Statesman, The Tribune, The Deccan Herald*, and *The Mirror*.

The author is grateful to the editors of these publications for first printing these articles.

CONTENTS

Acknowledgement	vii
Preface	xi
Pistols at Twenty Paces : A Duel at Poona	1
Colonel Gardner and the Princess of Cambay	3
The Lady of Sardhana	9
A Gentle Adventurer	16
The Company's Wines	19
Skinner and His Yellow Boys	22
The Story of "Bombay Church"	30
A Great Soldier : Benoit de Boigne	33
The Romance of the Mail Runner	44
Zoffany's *Last Supper*	47
Claude Martine : A Frenchman at the Court of Oudh	49
The Story of a Hill Station	56
A Hill Station's Vintage Murders	61
The Tomb and City of Tughlaq Shah	64
The Story of Karnal	67
An English Jester at the Moghul Court	70
Gems from a Bygone Age	73
Glories of the Hookah	77
Grandfather's Earthquake	81
Kipling's Simla	85
Bibliography	91

PREFACE

Professional historians will, I hope, forgive this intrusion into their domain by a mere story-teller. But so little has been written in recent times about those odd, colourful (and admittedly not very "great") soldiers of fortune — mostly European — who strutted across the Indian subcontinent during the eighteenth and nineteenth centuries, that I felt a sort of compulsion to resurrect and retell some of their more glorious (or inglorious) exploits — not so much because their lives throw some light on the times they lived in, and help us to understand manners, morals and values of Europeans and Asians during a period of colonial expansion.

Whatever else they may have been, these adventurers were individualists. They were not fighting for their country, or the East India Company, or even their paymasters — at least, not for long. They were fighting for their own hand, for their own enrichment, for their own greater glory — and sometimes, simply because they liked fighting.

Most of these chapters, together with the few pieces of more general interest, have appeared before — usually in a more condensed form — as articles in various newspapers and periodicals, including *The Illustrated Weekly of India, The Hindustan Times, The Times of India, The Sunday Standard, Hindusthan Standard, The Statesman* and *The Mirror*.

The Bibliography at the end gives a list of books I have consulted. Most of these are rare and out of print, and I found many of them not in public libraries, but during diligent searching in secondhand bookshops and private libraries in India.

I have visited most of the places described in this book, and have gone out of my way to see the smaller towns like Sardhana, Karnal, Aligarh and Bharatpur. History is best enjoyed in this way, by visiting the scene of actual events, and allowing one's imagination to roam backwards and forwards in time.

I am grateful to Kewlian Sio for writing to inform me, during the printing of this book, that on a corridor wall of St. Xavier's College in Bombay there is a water colour captioned 'Fr. Wendell receives a purse of money from Reinhard Sumro for enlarging the Jesuit church of Agra in 1772.' This must certainly be Sombre, alias Walter Reinhardt, the husband of Begum Samru.

RB

PISTOLS AT TWENTY PACES:
A DUEL AT POONA

DUELS AMONG British officers serving in India were fairly common in the early part of the nineteenth century, but we do not come across many accounts of them, as the penalties for duelling were severe. Such incidents were usually hushed up. And many of the "resignations" and sudden deaths from "cholera" were, in fact, the result of duels.

Perhaps the most tragic of these was the duel that was fought at Poona in June 1842. In that year the 27th Foot (Inniskillings), a North of Ireland regiment, whose officers were all Irish Protestants, was quartered at Poona. It had been some three months since an Irishman named Sarsfield, a mere boy of nineteen, belonging to an old and distinguished Catholic family, had been posted to the regiment. One of his ancestors had been James II's General at the Siege of Londonderry, and such ancestry and religion told against him in a Protestant regiment. His advent was looked upon as an insult to the regiment, and it was decided to make his life so intolerable that he would either resign or ask for a transfer to another regiment.

One night at the mess, Sarsfield, who had been drinking with the others, questioned a statement made by another officer, and, on being asked by the latter if he thought it was a lie, replied that he did. Immediately the other officer rose, bowed ceremoniously to Sarsfield, and left the mess-room in company with the paymaster. The others followed, leaving Sarsfield, who had a few more drinks before leaving and going home to bed.

At about four in the morning he was aroused by the paymaster, who brought him a challenge, or a demand for an apology. Not realising what he was doing, the young man dazedly signed the document the paymaster gave him, which was an abject apology. The next morning at six he appeared on parade, and, having but the faintest recollection of what had happened, walked up to the group of officers waiting for the parade to be formed. To his cheery good morning they returned a blank and contemptuous stare, and then, each turning on his heel, walked away. To give an apology was considered a most cowardly action.

For the next three months Sarsfield's life was miserable, for he was cut dead by everyone in the garrison. None spoke to him except on a matter of duty, and when he entered the mess, a dead silence fell over the company. The end came after three months, and there can be no doubt that the unfortunate young man was by now half demented.

One night he entered the mess-room, and, as usual, conversation ceased abruptly. There was a vacant seat immediately opposite the paymaster, and this Sarsfield took. By this time the conversation had been resumed, not the slightest notice being taken of him either by word or glance. He was waited upon by the servants just as the others were, and it was only as the table was being cleared for the second course that Sarsfield spoke.

"Will you take wine with me?" he said to the paymaster.

"I do not take wine with a coward," was the blunt reply.

"But you will take this?" was Sarsfield's rejoinder, as he dashed his wine-glass and its contents into the paymaster's face.

In a moment all were on their feet, and amidst a roar of voices Sarsfield was pulled out of the mess-room by the doctor.

"You will have to fight now, my boy," said the doctor, more sorrowfully than might have been expected.

"I know," said Sarsfield. "I came for that purpose."

The whole party now proceeded to a garden on the outskirts of the cantonment where such affairs were usually settled. All the preliminaries were quickly arranged, the captain acting as Sarsfield's second. It was a bright moonlit night, and the result was never for a moment in doubt, for the paymaster, at the first exchange of shots, put a bullet through Sarsfield's heart. Sarsfield did not fire. He had made no attempt to discharge his pistol.

The next issue of the *Poona Gazette* contained the following announcement:

"Suddenly, of cholera, in the officers' line of Her Majesty's 27th Foot, Ensign J.S. Sarsfield."

When an account of the circumstances reached Sarsfield's friends and relatives, a brother arrived at Poona and tried to ascertain the truth. But he could gain nothing more than what the doctor's certificate stated — "death by cholera" — for there was a mutual conspiracy of silence.

COLONEL GARDNER AND THE PRINCESS OF CAMBAY

OF THE MANY diverse Europeans who served in the armies of the Marathas, Colonel William Linnaeus Gardner was perhaps the most romantic and the most likeable. As a soldier he did not lack any of the dash or courage of George Thomas and James Skinner; but he was less flamboyant, a man of education and good taste, and if his life had its dramatic moments it was in spite of, rather than because of, his friendly disposition. His marriage to an Indian princess, though unusual and unorthodox, was an unqualified success.

The Victorian novelist Thackeray used the incidents of Gardner's life in sketching the career of his fictitious Major Gahagan, a swashbuckling character who was given to boasting about his exploits in India. The comparison was unfair, because there was no resemblance in character between the adventurer of fiction and the real man. But novelists are often very cruel, and will sometimes pillory their best friends if it enhances the interest of their work.

William Linnaeus Gardner, born in 1770, was a great-grandson of William Gardner of Coleraine, and a nephew of Alan, first Baron Gardner, an Irish peer and a distinguished Admiral in the British Navy. The boy was educated in France, and at the age of eighteen joined the British Army. In 1796 he landed at Calcutta with a company of the 30th Foot.

After an uneventful six months Gardner resigned his commission. At the time there was a certain amount of discontent among the English officers, some of whom resigned and entered the employment of Indian princes; but with Gardner it was probably just restlessness. He entered the service of Jaswant Rao Holkar, the great Maratha chief, and was one of the few officers who remained faithful to Holkar after the chief had lost his capital of Indore to his rival, Daulat Rao Sindhia. Holkar, finding it politic to come to terms with the British, against whom he had been intriguing for some time, sent Gardner as an emissary to Lord Lake. This was to be the beginning of a hair-raising adventure for Gardner. Many years later, relating his experiences to that indefatigable traveller and diarist, Lady Fanny Parkes, he said:

"One evening, when in Holkar's service, I was employed as an envoy to the Company's forces, with instructions to return within a certain time. My family remained in camp. Suspicion of treachery was caused by my lengthened absence, and accusations were brought forth against me at the durbar held by Holkar on the third day following that on which my presence was expected. I rejoined the camp while the durbar was in progress. On my entrance the Maharajah, in an angry tone, demanded the reason of my delay, which I gave, pointing out the impossibility of a speedier return. Whereupon Holkar exclaimed, in great anger, 'Had you not returned this day I would have levelled the *khanats* of your tent.' I drew my sword instantly and endeavoured to cut His Highness down, but was prevented by those around him; and before they had recovered from the amazement and confusion caused by the attempt, I rushed from the camp, sprang upon my horse, and was soon beyond the reach of recall."

The *khanats*, which caused so much indignation, were the canvas walls of Gardner's tent, which sheltered his newly-wedded wife, a Mohammedan princess of Cambay. Gardner was obviously head over heels in love with her. The threat of violating her privacy by pulling down her tent was taken by him as a mortal insult, and spurred the impulsive young officer to violent action. Fortunately for Gardner, his friends at the camp enabled his wife to join him afterwards. And Jaswant Rao did not prevent her from going after him: a strange act of generosity on his part, for he was soon afterwards to have all his European officers executed for suspected treachery; but the ways of a powerful Indian prince were unpredictable.

Gardner's marriage must have been one of the most romantic of his times. The marriage was conducted by Mohammedan rites. The lady was a thirteen-year-old princess of the house of Cambay, a state on the western seaboard of India. That engaging nosey-parker, Lady Fanny Parkes, elicited from Gardner this delightful account of his romantic union:

"When a young man, I was entrusted to negotiate a treaty with one of the native princes of Cambay. Durbars and consultations were continually held. During one of the former at which I was present, a curtain near me was gently pulled aside, and I saw, as I thought, the most beautiful black eyes in the world. It was impossible to think of the treaty: those bright and piercing glances, those beautiful dark eyes completely bewildered me.

"I felt flattered that a creature so lovely as she of those deep black, loving eyes should venture to gaze upon me. To what danger might not the veiled beauty be exposed should the movement of the purdah be seen by any of those present at the durbar? On quitting the assembly I discovered that the bright-eyed beauty was the daughter of the prince. At the next durbar my agitation and anxiety were extreme to again behold the bright eyes that haunted my dreams and my thoughts by day. The curtain was again gently waved, and my fate was decided.

"I demanded the princess in marriage. Her relations were at first indignant, and positively refused my proposal. However, on mature deliberation, the ambassador was considered too influential a person to have a request denied, and the hand of the young princess was promised. The preparations for the marriage were carried forward. 'Remember,' said I, 'it will be useless to deceive me. I shall know those eyes again, nor will I marry any other!'

"On the day of the marriage I raised the veil from the countenance of the bride, and in the mirror that was placed between us, in accordance with the Mohammedan wedding ceremony, I beheld the bright eyes that bewildered me. I smiled. The young Begum smiled too."

Gardner was sixty, and his wife living with him, when he gave this account to Lady Fanny; but his romantic ardour and love for his wife had not dimmed with the years. Few husbands, after forty years of marriage, would be as tender.

Gardner's adventures did not end when he fled from Holkar's camp. In his flight he fell into the hands of Amrit Rao, the Peshwa's intriguing brother, who suggested that Gardner enter his service to fight against the British in the Deccan. On Gardner's replying that he was not interested, he was tied to a cot, ready for execution; but as soon as he was unbound and marched off with his guard, he managed to make his escape, and threw himself off a cliff into a stream below, a drop of some fifty feet. He swam downstream until his guard had been eluded, disguised himself as a grass-cutter, and finally — after further wanderings — arrived at the British camp.

General Lake, who was soon to break the Maratha power near Delhi in 1803, gave Gardner a kind reception. Gardner's value and talents were obvious to him, and rather than lose him to another Indian chief, asked him to raise a corps of cavalry under the Company's flag. For its maintenance he was given the estate of Khasganj, in the Etah District of what is now Uttar Pradesh. His corps achieved a high reputation and became famous as "Gardner's Horse"; and Khasganj was to become the "country seat" of the heirs to an English Baronetcy.

It was at Khasganj that Gardner was joined by his wife after she left Holkar's camp. It was to be her home for the rest of her life; and in Khasganj — today a small, dusty, undistinguished village — both she and her husband were to die within a few months of each other.

But before retiring into the life of the "country gentleman" on his Khasganj estate, Gardner was to prove more than useful to the British. He had adopted an Indian way of life, he mixed freely with all kinds of Indians from princes and zamindars to poor farmers, soldiers and artisans, and his knowledge and understanding of the Indian character went deeper than any other Englishman's. The British were sensible enough to know the value of such a man; and Gardner was equally at ease in both worlds, and was popular with other British officers. Englishmen had not yet developed that social and moral priggishness which was to become characteristic of the Victorian era. Marrying a Moslem lady did not involve any social taboos, as it would have done fifty years later.

Unfortunately, Hindustan (as northern India was then known) was seething with anarchy: a condition which was "one of the main apologies for the appearance of British aggressiveness in the Indian peninsula". In Central India the Pindari freebooters were causing havoc; Rajputana was being bled to death by the Marathas; Oudh was a comic-opera scene of misgovernment and insecurity.

The beginning of 1814 saw Gardner preparing to enter Nepalese territory "in the peaceful capacity of a hunter and fisher, on a sporting expedition to the Dehra Dun", then held by the Nepalese. Here Gardner found himself in hot water. The Gurkhas had overrun most of Garhwal and Kumaon, including

Dehra, and they were naturally resentful of the Englishman's intrusion. Had they been able to get hold of him, he would have been shot as a spy; but the Mahant — the religious leader of a splinter Sikh community — sheltered him and helped him out of the valley.

War with Nepal came in November of the same year, and the Gurkhas' annexations proved to be their weakness rather than their strength. Gardner had pointed out that with an army of not more than 12,000 men the Gurkhas had to defend a frontier of 700 miles, stretching from Kathmandu, their capital, to Simla on the west. Between lay the beautiful sub-alpine region of Kumaon, its passes and glaciers themselves higher than any European mountains. The many rivers of Kumaon flow east and south until they join the Ganges, and the valleys form natural approaches to the region. On the fertile plateaux and uplands stood the principal Gurkha fort of Almora; but the garrison was weak, its troops were required elsewhere, and Gardner wrote to his superiors recommending its immediate occupation.

In the spring of 1815, while the British were still fumbling in the East and West, the Kumaon hills were invaded by a compact force of light infantry. At the head of his irregulars, Gardner attacked Almora and, though the Gurkhas defended resolutely, stormed the heights and carried the fort.

After more sporadic fighting, the Gurkhas evacuated Kumaon and later gave up their conquests west of the Jumna. After peace was made they became the most valued allies of the British and, together with the Sikhs, formed the hard fighting core of the Indian Army.

Gardner's brief campaign helped bring the Gurkha war to an early close; his conquest of Almora served to divide the Gurkha territories in two, and cut off their supply line. He was as good a negotiator as he was a soldier, and came to a quick understanding with his opponents once the fighting was over. It never took him very long to bridge the gulfs of race and religion.

His conquest of Almora also gave to India the first of her hill stations, where convalescent troops were sent, and civilians retreated to escape the heat of the plains. Later, Landour (Mussoorie), Ranikhet, Simla and Naini Tal were established. Not only did they become popular health resorts, but they were the centres of government business during the summer months.

In 1817 Gardner's irregular corps was incorporated with the

Company's cavalry; from "Gardner's Horse" the name was changed to the 2nd Bengal Cavalry; and it formed the nucleus of the famous Bengal Lancers.

The rest of his life was spent at Khasganj, only sixty miles from Agra. His Begum bore him two sons and a daughter. Each one made an interesting marriage. The eldest, James, married a niece of the Moghul Emperor, Akbar Shah. The younger son, Alan, was married to Bibi Sahiba Hinga, and left two daughters, Susan and Harmizi; the latter was married in 1836 to a relative, William Gardner, a nephew of the second Baron Gardner, and their son, Alan Hyde, succeeded to the title.

Nor did it end there. Alan Hyde Gardner, following in the footsteps of his grandfather, married Jane, daughter of Angam Shekoh, a converted princess of the House of Delhi, and had an heir, Alan Legge, born in 1881. To go any further into this interesting pedigree would only be inviting confusion; but Alan Legge never established his claim to the barony, and though today an heir must exist among the Gardners of Khasganj, the title has been allowed to lapse. Gardner's admirer, Lady Fanny Parkes, has given an interesting pedigree of the family up to 1850, showing the connection by intermarriage between the heirs and descendants of an English barony, the Imperial House of Taimur, the Kings of Oudh and the Princess of the Cambay.

THE LADY OF SARDHANA

THE BUS THAT TOOK US to Sardhana was prehistoric. I do believe it was kept from falling apart by a liberal use of sellotape. The noise and rattle made by its nuts and bolts and shaky chassis reminded me of Kipling's story "The Ship That Found Herself". Every part seemed alive and complaining. The bus conductor found the crank handle under somebody's seat, and, panting and sweating in the sun, kept turning it until, reluctantly, the engine spluttered into life. The bus moved off on its own volition, and the conductor just had time to get on and collect our tickets. Most of the passengers were rural folk, descendants of those Jats and Rohillas who made this fertile Doab region (the Doab is the area between the Ganges and the Jumna) one of the richest granaries of India, only to have it plundered by marauding Marathas, Sikhs and Afghans. They smoked *bidis* or chewed paan, shooting the coloured spittle out of the open windows; and, seeing my watch, asked me the time every few minutes.

The Sardhana bus stop, when we got to it, was the usual unexciting swamp of churned-up mud, with a tea stall, and several stray dogs and pigs nosing about in a garbage-heap. We hailed a cycle-rickshaw and told the man to take us to the church.

The Sardhana church was built at the expense of the Begum Samru by an Italian architect. Upon her husband's death she had become a devout Catholic, and earned from the Pope the title of "Joanna Nobilis". The Emperor at Delhi, grateful to her for services rendered in the battle-field, gave her another title: Zeb-un-Nissa, the "Ornament of her Sex". Her life, until she reached old age, was a succession of love affairs, intrigue, and petty warfare. It was never a dull life. She had certain admirable qualities which made her attractive to men. As a young girl, she was beautiful; in middle age, rather plump. She was a courageous woman, and rode into battle at the head of her troops, something which few women have done before or since. But we must begin at the beginning, and in the beginning was

Sombre, alias Samru, alias Walter Reinhardt. . . .

Sombre's real name was Walter Reinhardt, but due to a dusky complexion he acquired the name of Sombre, which in Hindustani was soon corrupted to Samru. He was perhaps the most notorious of foreign adventurers, and this notoriety was acquired when he was in the service of the Nawab of Bengal, Kassim Ali, who, warring with the English, had attacked and captured a large number of English residents at Patna, and ordered them to be executed.

None of Kassim's own native officers came forward to undertake this, but Sombre, wishing to ingratiate himself with his new employer, agreed to carry out the execution. Details of the murders are given in the Annual Register:

"Somers invited about forty officers and other gentlemen, who were amongst these unfortunate prisoners, to sup with him on the day he had fixed for the execution, and when his guests were in full security, protected as they imagined by the laws of hospitality, as well as by the right of prisoners, he ordered the Indians under his command to fall upon them and cut their throats. Even these barbarous soldiers revolted at the orders of this savage European. They refused to obey, and desired that arms should be given to the English, and that they would then engage them. Somers, fixed in his villainy, compelled them with blows and threats to the accomplishment of that odious service. The unfortunate victims, though thus suddenly attacked and wholly unarmed, made a long and brave defence, and with their plates and bottles even killed some of their assailants, but in the end they were all slaughtered. . . . Proceeding then, with a file of sepoys, to the prison where a number of prisoners then remained, he directed the massacre, and with his own hands assisted in the inhuman slaughter of 148 defenceless Europeans confined within its walls — an appalling act of atrocity that has stamped his name with infamy for ever."

Sombre left Kassim Ali's service before an avenging British army could catch up with him, and by the end of his subsequent career he had served twelve to fourteen masters. He finally tendered his services to Shah Alam, the Emperor of Delhi, who agreed to pay him Rs. 65,000 for his services and those of his two battalions. He remained in the service of the Delhi Court and was assigned a rich *jaghir*, or estate, at Sardhana, a district forty miles north of the capital, where he built and fortified his headquarters and settled down. He had adopted native dress, and the custom of keeping a harem.

At Sardhana he fell in love with a very beautiful woman. One historian asserts that she was the daughter of a decadent Moghul nobleman, another that she was a Kashmiri dancing girl, and a third that she was a lineal descendant of the Prophet. In due course she became Sombre's Begum. He died at Agra on the fourth of May 1778, aged fifty-eight years; infamous, unloved even by his own followers, but successful to the end.

After his death the command of his troops, their pay and the *jagir* of Sardhana became the property of his Begum, who, on being baptized and received into the Roman Catholic faith, was christened "Joanna Nobilis". By means of rare ability and force of character, she proved equal to her responsibilities; but she was unfortunate in her officers. Only the most dissolute had cared to join Sombre, and their conduct often incited the troops to mutiny. She gave the command to a German named Pauly "perhaps because he was a countryman of her husband, but, it has been suggested, for more tender reasons"; Pauly was murdered "by a bloody process" in 1783; and those who succeeded him did not remain long in command.

It was at this time that George Thomas, the Irish freelance, rose to a position of some importance in the army of Begum Samru.

When the Begum saw Thomas, it did not take her long to decide to give him a command. He had the pleasing, honeyed speech of the Irishman; he was tall, handsome, virile; far more attractive physically than most of the Europeans in her service. How could the Begum resist him? For months he would remain her most trusted officer, her lover, and then, seeking some other novelty, she would transfer her affections to another, only appealing to Thomas for help in time of distress.

This arrangement suited Thomas. He was willing to make love to the Begum without making the mistake of falling in love with her. He used her as she used him; but he never betrayed her, as she was often to betray him.

Several years after Thomas had left her service and had established himself at Panipat and Karnal, the Begum Samru, faced with a mutiny, appealed to him for help. She must have known Thomas's character well, for she had only recently raided his territory; any other person would have shown retaliation instead of succour; but when beauty was in distress Thomas always forsook his own interests to become the gallant knight-errant.

The Begum was now forty-five, inclined to plumpness, but her skin was still very smooth and fair, and her eyes "black, large and animated". The trouble at Sardhana had arisen from her having taken a new husband, a Frenchman named Le Vassoult.

Le Vassoult was no friend of Thomas's and had in fact proposed marriage to the Begum earlier, in order to gain an advantage over the Irishman who was then in her service. He was well educated and from an aristocratic family, but aloof by nature and unpopular with his men. A free and easy roisterer like Thomas got more from his troops than the conventional disciplinarian. Both officers and troops resented the fact that Le Vassoult, after his marriage to the Begum, refused to eat with them or treat them as equals; they planned on deposing the Begum and transferring their allegiance to Balthazar Sombre, a debauched son of Sombre by his first wife. This first wife was still alive, and when she died in 1838 she must have been over a hundred years old. (The Sardhana cemetery contains the remains of many centenarians.)

Another officer named Legois, a friend of George Thomas, had tried to dissuade the Begum from raiding Thomas's territory in Hariana, and for this had been badly treated by Le Vassoult. The troops, who had served Legois for a long time, and obviously liked him, broke into mutiny, and the Begum and her husband had no alternative but to try and reach Anupshahr, then the last outpost of British territory in northern India.

The troops had sent for Balthazar Sombre from Delhi. Le Vassoult and the Begum slipped away, but were soon pursued and overtaken. The lovers had agreed that rather than fall into the hands of the mutineers they would first kill themselves. While Le Vassoult, an unimaginative man of honour, was quite serious about this pact, the Begum treated it lightly. On being surrounded, she drew a dagger and made a half-hearted attempt at stabbing herself; but all she did was nick her breast and bespatter her blouse with blood. Le Vassoult was more thorough. On hearing that the Begum was bleeding to death, he drew his pistol, put the muzzle to his mouth, and pulled the trigger.

"The ball passed through his brain, and he sprang from the saddle a full foot in the air, before he fell dead to the ground. His corpse was subjected to every indignity and insult that the gross and bestial imagination of his officers and men could conceive, and left to rot, unburied, on the ground."

However, the Begum did not get off too lightly. She was taken back to Sardhana and chained between two guns, occasionally being placed astride one of them at mid-day, when it was nearly red hot. The only food she received was smuggled to her by her maid-servants. This was the Begum's plight when Thomas, by forced marches, reached Sardhana and quelled the mutiny.

The command of the Begum's force was now given to Colonel Saleur (the only European who could write) and he and the others signed or affixed their seals to a document in which they swore allegiance to their mistress. This was drawn up by a Mohammedan scribe in Persian, and as his religion prevented him from acknowledging Christ as God, the document was superscribed: "In the name of God, and of His Majesty Christ!"

In 1803, after the British had defeated the Marathas, and established themselves in Hindustan (then the name for most of northern India) the Begum submitted to General Lake near Agra. James Skinner, the famous Eurasian adventurer, left a description of her meeting with the General: "When the Begum came in person to pay her respects to General Lake, an incident occurred of a curious and characteristic description. She arrived at headquarters just after dinner, and being carried in her palanquin at once to the reception tent, the General came out to meet and receive her. As the adhesion of every petty chieftain was, in those days, of consequence, Lord Lake was not a little pleased at the early demonstration of the Begum's loyalty, and being a little elevated by the wine which had just been drunk, he forgot the novel circumstance of its being a native female, instead of some well-bearded chief, so he gallantly advanced, and, to the utter dismay of her attendants, took her in his arms and kissed her. The mistake might have been awkward, but the lady's presence of mind put all right. Receiving courteously the proferred attention, she turned calmly around to her astonished attendants and observed, 'It is the salute of a priest to his daughter'."

When the Begum accepted British protection, her income increased, and she disbanded most of her troops. Bishop Heber saw her in 1825 and described her as a "very queer looking old woman, with brilliant but wicked eyes, and the remains of beauty in her features".

She became very rich and philanthropic. She sent the Pope at Rome Rs. 150,000, the Archbishop of Canterbury Rs. 50,000. She built a church at Meerut — less pretentious but more handsome than the one at Sardhana — where the Roman Catholic bishop was an Italian named Julius Caesar. At Meerut she often entertained Governors-General and Commanders-in-Chief, and when she died in 1836, at the age of ninety, she left behind a fortune of £700,000 and an immense army of pensioners.

The Sardhana church hasn't changed much over the years. The dome is nobly proportioned, but the twin spires on either side somehow spoil the effect. They are not spires actually, but pyramidal structures that serve no purpose, aesthetic or practical. The interior of the church is handsome, and has several new additions; but the centre of interest are the eleven life-size statues and three panels in bas-relief. This marble monument is the work of an Italian sculptor, Adamo Tadolini of Bologna. The Begum in her rich dress is seated on a chair of state holding in her right hand a folded scroll, the Emperor's *firman* conferring on her the *Jagir* of Sardhana. On her right stands Dyce Sombre, her step-son, and on her left Dewan Rae Singh, her Minister. Immediately behind are Bishop Julius Caesar and Innayat Ullah, her commandant of cavalry.

Of the three panels one represents an incident in the consecration of the church when she presented rich vestments to the Bishop (these are still in existence). The other panel shows the Begum holding a durbar, surrounded by European officers; and the third shows the Begum mounted on an elephant in triumphant procession.

We felt like intruders, our footsteps resounding in the silent church, and we did not stay long. There was nothing else to see except the Begum's palace, now a school, and a few old houses and graves. The spirit of the Begum's time has left Sardhana, and it is just another district town, hot and dusty and malarious.

It is difficult to believe that there was drama here once, intrigue, battle and romance. The place is a backwater, cut off somehow from the mainstream of life. A few nuns pass through the church cloisters, and a bullock-cart trundles along the road. The fields are waterlogged.

We went away before sunset, afraid that if we stayed too long we might meet the ghost of a queer-looking old woman with brilliant and wicked eyes, lurking in the mango-grove near the church.

A GENTLE ADVENTURER

THE SECOND HALF of the eighteenth century in India was a period of anarchy and confusion. The Moghul Empire was rapidly disintegrating; the old and blind Emperor at Delhi owed his throne to the Marathas, who controlled most of northern India; the Sikhs and Rohillas worried Delhi from the north; and in the south and east the British were steadily expanding their territory. It was a period of lawlessness, when individual men rose to positions of great power, and freebooters and adventurers made themselves rich. There were many European adventurers who served Marathas or Jats or Moghuls. Most of them were deserters — crude, avaricious, without scruple; but there was one, forgotten today, who was not only a soldier but a gentle dreamer.

It is to Colonel Tod, author of *The Annals of Rajasthan*, that we owe what information we have about Thomas Legge. It was to Tod's tent in the Rajasthan desert that the tired, wounded adventurer found his way.

Legge was a native of northern Ireland. He was wild in his youth and, running away from home, joined the *Swallow*, a sloop of war bound for Madras. Arriving in India, he deserted his ship (this was the accepted procedure for a young man who sought his fortune abroad) and tramped all the way to Hyderabad, in Sind, a distance of some two thousand miles, supporting himself on the way by begging. This was about 1775.

Tom Legge remained in the lower Indus districts for five or six years, and then began a long series of wanderings: to Multan in the Punjab, and from there through the desert to Jaipur. After a short period as a gunsmith in the service of the Jat Rana of Gohad, Legge was on his way again, eventually reaching Kabul, where his knowledge of guns gained him a job on a salary of three rupees a day.

He remained several years at Kabul, where he was both useful and popular; but the wanderlust returned, and slipping out of Kabul, he journeyed north, over the Hindu Kush, to Bokhara. He visited Herat and Kandahar, and spent twenty years "serving almost every power between the Indus and the Caspian". Eventually tiring of a nomadic existence, he decided to return to Jaipur, where he meant to settle down permanently.

At Jaipur, Tom Legge married a daughter of the celebrated Favier de Silva, who had been sent to India by the King of Portugal to assist Jai Singh, the ruler of Jaipur, in his astrological studies. Later, at Delhi and at Jaipur, the prince built his famous observatories.

Through this marriage, Thomas Legge obtained command of a battalion in the Jaipur army, but his first command was his last. While storming the fort of a rebel chief, he was twice wounded, and after the battle was over and the vultures were settling down, he found his way to Colonel Tod's camp, where he hoped to obtain medical assistance.

"I was poked down with a pike, and shot through my thigh, and I've come to your honour's camp to get cured, for they can make no hand at it at Jaipur," were his words to Colonel Tod.

He stayed at the British camp for some months, and during his stay told the Colonel many stories connected with his travels.

Tom Legge was an unusual and unconventional man. He practised alchemy and divination, and his wonderful memory was a fount for the legends of Central Asia. He also suffered from a delusion that during his wanderings he had discovered the Garden of Eden. It was approached by a road leading through dark caverns, and guarded by an angel with flaming wings. The garden lay deep in the heart of a mountain; it was filled with delicious fruit and piles of gold and silver bricks. This fantasy of Legge's illustrated the two sides to his character: the garden, the angels and the fruit showed him to be a gentle visionary, the gold and silver bricks were what all adventurers dreamed of. Tom Legge insisted that he had found the Garden of Eden somewhere in the Hindu Kush. And who can refute him? It may, indeed, be there.

His wound did not heal, and he began to waste away.

"I fear not death," he told Colonel Tod, "and could I get my life written and my boy sent to Calcutta, I should die contented."

He decided to return to Jaipur, but had not gone far from the camp when he was overcome by a mood of deep despair and, throwing away his clothes, entered a deserted tomb, where he began to live like a fakir. Here he was discovered by the wife of

Sindhia's general, Jean Baptiste Filoze. She tried to help him, but it was too late, and Tom Legge died soon after he was removed from the tomb in which he had made his abode.

That was in the year 1808. His son did indeed go to Calcutta, but what became of him there is not known. The story of Tom Legge's life was never written, and we would not have heard of him at all had he not stumbled into the tent of a great historian on a hot, windy afternoon in the desert, one hundred and fifty years ago.

THE COMPANY'S WINES

THERE IS HISTORICAL precedent for relaxing the prohibition laws for at least some people in parts of the country. While doing some reading the other day, I made the interesting discovery that the Emperor Akbar published a decree permitting intoxicating spirits to be sold to Europeans because, he said, "they are born in the element of wine, as fish are produced in that of water . . . and to prohibit them the use of it is to deprive them of life".

Akbar's son and successor, Jehangir, was by his heavy drinking to prove conclusively that it was not only Europeans who took to wine as fish do to water. But it is true that when the East India Company first obtained a foothold in India the Englishman's appetite for food and drink was enormous. The traveller, Albert de Mandelslo, who visited Surat in 1638, tells us that at dinner, which was taken at midday, fifteen or sixteen dishes of meat, besides dessert, appeared on the table. At that period the usual cold beverages were Spanish sack, Persian wines, English beer and pale punch.

The seventeenth century in India may be said to have been the age of punch. For almost a century punch was drunk by every European; to excess, by most of them. The factors of Surat favoured hot drinks rather than cold, and are said to have been the inventors of punch, the name being derived from the Hindustani "panch" (five), which stood for the drink's five ingredients — spirits, lemon-juice, spices, sugar and water. The spirit used was arrack — distilled in India from various things, such as the fermented sap of palm trees, sugarcane juice, rice, or even, according to one writer, from seaweed, so abundant on the island of Bombay. Arrack made from seaweed was known as Fool's Rack — for obvious reasons. . . . Another favourite hot drink was "burnt wine", made by boiling wine with spices. This was drunk in the morning, piping hot, to comfort the stomach.

The mortality among the early English settlers was extremely high everywhere except at Surat (where, apparently, the climate favoured heavy drinking). At Harrapur, where the first English factory in Bengal was founded in 1638, five out of the six factors stationed there were dead within the year. This high mortality was attributed to the abundance of arrack at that place. In Bombay, two monsoons was the average life expectancy of an Englishman in the seventeenth century.

The difficulty and expense of importing European wines led to the use of too much arrack, especially among the East India Company's young writers and soldiers. High prices, however, did not affect more wealthy members of society, and it was usual for a man to take his three bottles of claret after dinner every day, in addition to the Madeira which he took during the meal. A lady drank, on an average, one bottle of wine a day. Much of this wine had to be taken in honouring the many toasts which were constantly being proposed at dinners, tiffins and breakfasts. At private tables it was expected that the host and hostess would take wine with each guest, and that every guest would do the same with the others present. When all these toasts had been drunk, there were still a few other "sentiments" with which to conclude the drinking.

Punch drinking was popular well into the eighteenth century. In 1707 there were seven licensed punch houses in the small settlement of Calcutta. These houses were often the scenes of brawls which occasionally ended in bloodshed: a sword was an indispensable part of a gentleman's dress. Punch houses continued to exist in India until the nineteenth century, although by that time people began to realise that punch and the Indian climate did not go well together. This did not make them teetotallers. Instead they took to drink that was milder than arrack, and the Wine Age in India had commenced.

The prices of wine were cheap — Old Red Port being Rs 16 per dozen, and Fine Old Sherry Rs 14; whilst Burton Ale was Rs 10 a dozen, a Country Bottled Ale Rs 7 a dozen.

Soda water was not introduced into Calcutta until 1812, its price being Rs 14 per dozen — the same as good sherry! When a cargo of ice from America arrived in 1833, it was sold at 4 annas (current twenty-five paise) per seer (pound).

From the mid-nineteenth century beer began to replace wine; this was country beer, as English beer was considered too "liverish" for India. The age of brandy succeeded that of beer. Brandy's popularity was probably due to the introduction of ice and soda water: brandy with warm water was not considered a very inviting drink. In northern India the nights during the winter were sufficiently cold to cause ice to form in shallow trays of water; it was stored in pits for use in the hot weather. But Calcutta rarely saw ice before 1833, when a cargo of apples arrived there, packed in ice. It scalded the backs of the coolies who carried it ashore, and fetched a higher price than the apples.

Soda water was introduced and manufactured in India in about 1835 (ice was first manufactured here a few years later) and was soon found in every Englishman's house. Brandy and soda remained the most popular drink for thirty years. The era of the whisky-and-soda dates from the seventies. To quote Douglas Dewar, "Even as Bridge suddenly and completely ousted Whist, so has whisky supplanted brandy."

For those who can afford it, whisky still reigns supreme. Rum, they say, is for soldiers, gin for women, and beer for schoolboys. But there is nothing to compare with the British soldier's condiment, "Fixed Bayonets" — a chicken stuffed with chillies and boiled in rum!

SKINNER AND HIS YELLOW BOYS

ONE OF THE MOST historic churches in India is the church of St. James, near the Kashmere Gate, just within the walls of old Delhi. Few know that its builder, James Skinner, was a Eurasian who first served in the army of the Marathas, and later raised a famous cavalry corps, known as Skinner's Horse (or the "Yellow Boys", because of their canary-coloured uniforms) for the Company's army. But he was a man of many parts. Just across the road from St. James was a small mosque said to have been built by Skinner for Muslim members of his family; and it is said that he built a temple, too — his mother was a Hindu — but its whereabouts are not known today. Close behind the mosque, now hidden from the street by shops, is the decaying mansion that Skinner built as his Delhi residence.

James Skinner was born in 1778. His father was a Scotsman, an officer in the Company's service, and his mother the daughter of a Rajput landholder from Mirzapur. She was taken prisoner by the British in a war with the Raja of Benares, and came under the protection of Ensign Skinner, to whom in due course she bore six children, three sons and three daughters. David, the eldest, went to sea; James, the second, became a military adventurer; and Robert, the youngest, was to follow in his footsteps.

Skinner's mother committed suicide in 1790, because her daughters were sent to that dreaded institution, School. This, for her, was a violation of the sanctity of purdah, and her Rajput honour was sullied. After her death, the boys were sent to a charity school. The father was still only a lieutenant, and could not afford to give them an expensive education. But when he was promoted to a captaincy in 1793, he immediately sent his sons to a good boarding-school, where the fee was Rs. 30 a month; quite high for those days of cheap living, when the poor were very poor and the rich were very rich. Two years later James was apprenticed to a printer in Calcutta.

Three days of the printing office were enough for the restless and high-spirited young Skinner. On the fourth day he ran away, with six annas in his pocket. It says something for the cost of living in eighteenth century Calcutta that, limiting himself to spending only one anna a day, Skinner managed to live on six annas for six days. His money finished, he wandered about the bazaars of Calcutta, working at anything that came his way.

For a week he carried loads with the poorest of coolies; then he picked up a modest wage — three annas a day — by pulling the drill for an Indian carpenter. One day he was spotted by a servant of his elder sister, and dragged off to his brother-in-law's house, but an understanding godfather, Colonel Burn, gave the youngster Rs 300 and sent him to Kanpur where Skinner's father's regiment was stationed.

A fortnight later Colonel Burn — godfathers once took their duties seriously — arrived at Kanpur, and gave Skinner a letter of introduction to no less a person than General de Boigne, who was at Aligarh. A commission under de Boigne could make the career and fortune of a young adventurer.

De Boigne soon retired, and Skinner found himself serving under General Perron, another Frenchman. The first outstanding action in which he took part was the battle of Malpura, outside Jaipur. Skinner nearly lost his own life in repulsing the Rathor cavalry; his horse was killed under him, and he escaped by means of a rather undignified retreat under a tumbril.

After the battle Skinner was the first to enter the Jaipur camp. Here he admits to having looted two golden idols with diamond eyes belonging to Raja Partap Singh, and trinkets to the value of Rs 2,000, amongst them "a brass fish, with two *chowrees* hanging down like moustachios." This turned out to be the *Mahi Maratib*, or the Fish of Dignities, a decoration conferred by Moghul Emperors on rajas of a very high rank, and "equivalent to the Three Horse Tails of the Turkish Empire, or the Button of the Chinese mandarin". Skinner did not keep these acquisitions for himself, but presented them to his Maratha general; and in return he was given the traditional *khilat*, or dress of honour.

Skinner's most exciting and dangerous engagement took place when he was ordered to assist the Karaoli raja against his neighbour of Uniara. The Karaoli force consisted of six battalions of infantry, 2,000 cavalry, and twenty guns, but the only efficient troops were Skinner's.

The two armies met somewhere between Tonk and the Chambal river, but before this the Karaoli chief's troops had mutinied because he had been unable to pay them. Skinner sent for reinforcements; but, before any could arrive, the Uniara raja, deciding to strike while the iron was hot — or better still, to make it hot by striking — moved out to give battle. The result was that the entire Karaoli infantry deserted to the enemy, and only Skinner's battalion was left to face them.

Skinner immediately made a retreat towards a deserted village in his rear, driving off two of the enemy's battalions, which had charged. Then the entire Uniara cavalry and infantry, some 6,000 men, attacked him. Skinner realised that it was hopeless to try to hold the village. He decided to retreat to Tonk, about six miles distant; but before he could begin his retreat, he was attacked by the two battalions who had previously charged him and were now aided by their cavalry. In repulsing them, Skinner lost one of his five guns, and again his horse was killed under him. The rest of the enemy were now coming up fast, and further movement was impossible. Drawing up his men on the level plain, Skinner "made them a short but spirited speech, telling them they could die but once, and exhorting them to fight, and, if needs be, fall like good and brave soldiers".

Allowing the enemy to come within his range of fifty yards, Skinner gave them a volley, then charged. The enemy gave way, and he captured their guns; "but their flanks wheeled into action and galled him terribly"; Skinner threw his men into a square and attempted to reach some ravines about a mile distant. But he was not given the chance. Encouraged by his retreat, the enemy charged time and again, captured three more of his guns, and killed so many of his men that he was left with only 300. Desperately he called on these few to make a final effort, but as he was leading them forward he was shot through the groin by a matchlock man, and fell unconscious. The remnants of his very gallant battalion were completely destroyed.

He fell at three o'clock in the afternoon, and did not regain consciousness till next morning. He had been taken for dead, and robbed of everything except his pantaloons. "Around him," writes Herbert Compton in a graphic account of the battle, "were heaps of his dead and wounded native officers and soldiers, among them a Subahdar with his leg shot off below the knee, and a Jemadar with a pike thrust through his body. All were tortured with thirst, and unable to move; and thus they remained in helpless agony through the long hot day, praying for death. Night came at last, but neither relief from suffering nor assistance. The moon was full and clear, and about midnight it was very cold. So dreadful did the night appear that Skinner vowed to himself that if he survived it he would never go soldiering again, and if he lived to recover, that he would build a church to the god of his white father. The wounded on all sides were moaning and crying out for water, and the jackals kept flitting about like four-legged ghouls, tearing the dead, and coming closer and closer to the living, and were only kept off by stones feebly thrown at them."

On the second morning an old man and woman from a neighbouring village came to the battlefield with a basket and jar of water. The woman offered a piece of bread and a drink of water to every wounded man. This was gratefully accepted by Skinner, but as the woman was a *Chumarin* (an untouchable) the Subahdar, a high-caste Rajput, would take nothing from her hands, saying that a little more suffering was nothing and that he preferred to die unpolluted.

A party of the Uniara raja's men eventually rescued Skinner and the other wounded. The stubborn Subahdar now received water from acceptable hands and, to Skinner's delight, recovered; and he and Skinner and the others "were lifted in sheets" and taken to the raja's camp.

After a month, during which he was hospitably treated by the Uniara raja, Skinner was freed. Wars were then conducted in a gentlemanly fashion, though during the fighting itself no quarter was given. He did not forget the kindness of the *Chumarin* woman, and soon after sent her a present of a thousand rupees, together with the message that he considered her as his mother.

A few months later — after a period of leave in Calcutta, where he stayed with his sister — Skinner was again on active service, this time against that swashbuckling Irishman, George Thomas, who had carved out a kingdom of his own over an area of some 200 square miles in the Hariana region of what is now the Punjab. He posed a threat to the power of Perron in Hindustan and, but for his fits of drunkenness, might well have gained control over Delhi.

Both James and his younger brother Robert Skinner fought together in the battle of Georgegarh (Thomas's fortress, known today as Jhajgarh in the Rohtak District), where the Irishman held out gallantly against a numerically superior foe. An incident occurred during the fighting which showed the close ties that bound Skinner to his brother.

Baillie Fraser, Skinner's biographer and translator (James Skinner penned his memoirs in Persian), writes: "James and Robert Skinner were engaged at different parts of the field, so that neither knew how the other fared. The cannonade was so fierce and continuous, and the slaughter so great, that all was smoke and carnage and there was little communication between the different battalions engaged. When the battle ceased, a report came to James that his brother had been killed, whilst a similar one reached Robert as to James. Both, moved by one impulse, ran to the bloody field, without thinking of rest or refreshment, and sought all over for the body of the brother, but in the darkness, amidst the thousands of corpses, torn and mutilated by the cannon shot, neither found what he sought, and after a weary and fruitless search they returned to the tent of their commanding officer to make their report. By a singular chance they entered from opposite sides at the same moment, and the first thing that met their eyes was the object on which their thoughts were dwelling. They saw nothing else, but ran and embraced, calling out each other's names before the officers that filled the tent."

In the hand to hand fighting that took place later at George Thomas's capital of Hansi, Robert Skinner found himself face to face with Thomas, a giant of a man, and took a swipe at him with his sword. Thomas was saved by his armoured vest; later, after his surrender, he "was particularly gracious to the younger Skinner, whom he embraced, and showed him the cut he had received from him on his belt". When the Marathas were defeated by the British in 1803, and Sindhia's European officers disbanded, Robert Skinner took service with the private army of Begum Samru, Thomas's old mistress.

When war broke out between Daulat Rao Sindhia and the British in August 1803, all British subjects in the Maratha army were dismissed from service. Skinner protested his loyalty and tried to get the dismissal order reversed. Seeing Perron bareheaded and "riding about endeavouring to rally his horsemen" — Lake had drawn up his army just outside the fort of Aligarh — Skinner ran to him, seized his bridle, and made a last offer of service to the distracted General.

"Ah! No," cried Perron. "All is over. Those fellows have behaved badly. Do not ruin yourself. Go over to the English; it is all up with us."

Skinner renewed his assurances of loyalty, but Perron shook him off and rode away, crying, "Goodbye, Monsieur Skinner. No trust, no trust!"

"Then you can go to the devil!" roared Skinner, finally losing his patience.

A few days later Skinner rode into General Lake's camp, unsure of his reception because of the colour of his skin; but Lake had a weakness — or rather an admiration — for most military adventurers, and just as he had received Gardner two years earlier, so he received Skinner. So great a fancy did he take to the Eurasian that, when 2,000 of Perron's Hindustani horse came over to the English after the battle of Delhi, Skinner was given their command. The troopers, given a choice of the various English officers who had come over from Sindhia's army, at once chose Skinner, shouting "Sikander Sahib!" without any hesitation.

His name, corrupted to Is-kinner by the troops, had become Sikander, the Hindustani name for Alexander the Great: a compliment to Skinner's courage and military qualities. Skinner adopted a canary-coloured uniform for his cavalry corps, called Skinner's Horse, though more popularly known as the Yellow Boys. Soon his irregular cavalry was patrolling the northern borders.

When a few years later the British, very temporarily, adopted a policy of "non-intervention" in the affairs of Indian States, Skinner "beat his sabre into a pruning-hook" and settled down as a farmer on his estates in Hariana, where he had once fought against George Thomas. He was so successful in settling these Districts that he was rewarded with a grant of sixty-seven farms in and around Hansi for the maintenance of his troops. In addition he held an estate of his own, acquired when he was in Sindhia's service, at a small place called Bilaspur, in the Bulandshahr district, some thirty-five miles from Delhi.

In 1815 Skinner belted on his sword once more, and he and his Yellow Boys distinguished themselves against the Pindari marauders; then against the Arab mercenaries who revolted at

Poona in 1819. After this, most of his men went into cantonment at Hansi. Only once again, in the restless '20s, were Skinner and his Yellow Boys called upon in an emergency. According to H. G. Keene in *Hindustan Under the Freelances,* "a sort of magnetic storm brooded over the land, causing unrest and reaction. The upper provinces were full of soldiers whose occupation was gone, and whose habits forbade their finding new work in peaceful fields. . . . The administration of justice was imperfect and universally unpopular" (especially in those districts which had known the superior administrative talents of de Boigne); "worst of all, the settlement of the land — always the cornerstone of the Indian social system — was crude, corrupt and unworkable."

There were pre-Mutiny rumblings, local disturbances everywhere — in the Cis-Sutlej country, the Doab, Rajputana; and the famous Jat State of Bharatpur, never completely subdued by the British, was once again in arms owing to a disputed succession; and as already mentioned Skinner's Horse, with their commander at their head, took part in the ensuing five weeks' siege of Bharatpur.

Then finally, a Lieutenant-Colonel in the British Army, he retired to Hansi with his men. He had still many years left to live, and it appears that he spent these actively, increasing his family considerably. His domestic habits were more Mohammedan than Christian, and he left behind him children by at least fourteen wives.

In fulfilment of the vow he made on the battlefield of Uniara, to build a church if his life was spared, he built St. James at Delhi, at a cost of £20,000. At the same time he built a mosque for the use of his wives; and, it is said, a temple in honour of his mother.

Skinner was a modest, unassuming man, devoted to his family and to the welfare of his men. Though he became quite English in his habits, he was more at ease writing in Persian than in English. His memoirs were written in Persian; so was an ode to the heir of the Begum Samru, in which he attempted to dissuade the young man from visiting England.

Skinner died in December 1841 of a heart attack brought on by a bowel obstruction and too liberal dosings of every variety of purgative. It was possible for him to survive a hundred fierce battles, but far more difficult to survive his doctors, who administered the doses. He was buried at Hansi, with full military honours, but later his remains were taken to Delhi where, according to his wishes, they were placed under the door sill of St. James, so that all who entered might "trample upon the chief of sinners", as he unworthily chose to describe himself.

On the seventeenth of January 1842, accompanied by his eldest son, his entire corps, and a great crowd of people, Skinner's body was taken from Hansi to Sitaram ka Sarai, on the outskirts of Delhi. Here the cortege was met by the civilians and officers of the British cantonment, and then, accompanied by a vast crowd from the city, Skinner's coffin was carried to his church.

"None of the Emperors of Hindustan," wrote an Urdu scribe afterwards, "were ever brought into Delhi in such state as Sikander Sahib!"

THE STORY OF "BOMBAY CHURCH"

AS YOU ENTER St. Thomas' Cathedral in Bombay, and look at the memorial tablets and monuments that cover the walls, you are at once taken back over two hundred years, to the time when Bombay was first settled by the merchants and factors of the East India Company. The Company had rented the island of Bombay for £10 a year, from King Charles II, who had received it as part of the dowry of Catherine of Braganza, the Portuguese princess.

Sir Gerald Aungier, President of the East India Company's factories, was virtually the ruler of Bombay in those halcyon days. He improved the island's fortifications, quelled a mutiny, and built up a strong garrison force. The church was begun by him in 1672, but interest in it flagged, and it was not until 1718, some time after Aungier's death, that it was finally completed. This was due mainly to the enthusiasm and zeal of the Rev. Richard Cobbe.

When Cobbe arrived at Bombay as chaplain to the island, he found that services were held in a room in the fort. In his sermons he impressed on the congregation the necessity of a suitable church.

"Well, Doctor Cobbe," said the Governor, after attending a service, "you have been very zealous for the church this morning."

"Yes, your honour," replied Cobbe, "I think there was occasion for it, and I hope without offence."

"Well, if we must have a church, we must have a church," said the Governor. "Do you get a book made, and see what everyone will contribute towards it."

Cobbe himself gave over a thousand rupees. Other donors included a certain Cornelius Toddington who gave twenty rupees, "For my wife, when I have her." A substantial sum was collected, and a foundation stone was laid. Three years later, on Christmas day, the church opened. The Governor arrived in procession, and after the service he accompanied the ladies and his Council to the vestry, where they drank success to the new church in the choicest sack and sherry.

The church prospered under Cobbe's administration, but he was soon quarrelling with the Governor's Council, and making its members the subjects of criticism in his sermons. As one cannot indulge too freely in libel, even from a pulpit, Cobbe found himself suspended from the Company's service and debarred from officiating as chaplain. He returned to England, and lived to an advanced age.

Until a diocese was founded and other churches gradually built, the church was known everywhere as "Bombay Church", and was the one place of worship for English merchants living in Bombay. James Forbes in his *Oriental Memoirs* gives us a charming picture of the Green in front of the church in 1763.

"A company of soldiers is drawn up before the church. A gentleman with cocked hat, knee-breeches, and a long stick, with a servant holding an umbrella over his head, is gazing at them. A coach, drawn by four horses, preceded by a company of sepoys, is being driven past the church. A factor is being carried in an open palanquin, flanked by two sepoys with drawn swords. There is a gentleman riding in a chaise and pair", as a bullock-cart was then styled! The bullocks would "trot and gallop as well as horses, and are equally serviceable in every respect — except that they sometimes incommode by the filth thrown upon you by their tails". An officer in full-dress uniform, driving about Bombay in a small bullock-cart, must have been a striking though not unusual sight in old Bombay.

In 1836 the church became the cathedral of the diocese, and the low belfry was converted into a high tower. An extensive programme of rebuilding was begun twenty-five years later, but had to be curtailed because of the trade depression that overtook the local merchants following the end of the American Civil War. The chancel and sanctuary were the results of this scheme of rebuilding, and were executed in ornate pseudo-Gothic; but the nave and western part of the church are early works, and possess both dignity and elegance.

The large number of monuments inside the cathedral reflect a great deal of the history of Bombay: a monument to Jonathan Duncan (1811), Governor for sixteen years, shows him receiving the blessings of a young Hindu — a reference to Duncan's efforts at suppressing infanticide in some districts near Benares and in Kathiawar; to Colonel Burn, who commanded at the battle of Kirkee (1817); to Colonel John Campbell, defender of Mangalore against Tippu in 1784; to John Carnac (1780), who served with Clive in Bengal, and his wife Eliza Rivett, whose portrait by Reynolds is in the Wallace Collection in London; to Admiral Maitland (1839), who received Napoleon aboard the *Bellerophon;* and a host of others.

Hemmed in as it is today by the bustle and noise of modern Bombay, it is difficult to imagine St. Thomas' as it must have looked two hundred years ago, dominating the centre of the spacious Bombay Green; but enter its walls, and the world is at once hushed, and it is possible to forget the shops and blocks of offices outside; and, running our hands over the old stones and worn marble, we feel the presence of those merchant adventurers who turned an unhealthy, malarious island into a great port and a teeming metropolis.

A GREAT SOLDIER : BENOIT DE BOIGNE

"MY PAST APPEARS a dream!" exclaimed General de Boigne towards the end of his life, when he lived far, far from the India he had known so well. And to us, it does seem like a dream, but de Boigne's achievements were so very real that the course of Indian history might well have been altered but for the premature death of his master, Madhavrao Sindhia, and de Boigne's subsequent withdrawal from the country.

Aligarh, today, is a town of many contrasts. There is the old city of Koil, with its narrow, insanitary lanes, infested with flies by day and mosquitoes by night. There is the cantonment area, with the old mansions and spacious grounds, many of them built over a hundred years ago by Sindhia's French officers; and outside the town are hundreds of villages scattered throughout the district, where wheat, sugarcane, maize and gram have been cultivated since Moghuls, Marathas, Jats, Afghans and Rohillas each swept over the fertile plains of this important district of northern India.

At that time every man was a law unto himself. An official record, compiled a century later, tells us that "in those days (the reign of Shah Alam) the highways were unoccupied and travellers walked through byways. The facility of escape, the protection afforded by heavy jungles and the numerous forts that then studded the country, with the ready sale for plundered property, all combined to foster spoilation". Eventually Aligarh was taken by Madhavrao Sindhia, the Maratha chieftain, who had gained control over most of Hindustan (then the name for northern India), and held it until the British vanquished his successor.

Aligarh became the headquarters of Sindhia's army, organized, trained and maintained by a French soldier of fortune, Benoit de Boigne. It was during the association between Sindhia and de Boigne that the Marathas held complete sway over northern India. De Boigne was perhaps the only European officer in the service of an Indian chief who left the country in a blaze of honour and glory. One of the most able and at the same time benevolent generals of his time, he introduced into his districts the first forms of civil administration.

He was born on the eighth of March 1751 at Chambery in Savoy, a principality then owing allegiance to the King of Sardinia. It is difficult to say whether Benoit — his real name was Le Borgne — was Italian or French. Though a subject of the King of Sardinia, his parents were French, owners of a fur shop in Chambery; in later life he was to become a British subject; but he never fought for French or British, and his standard, when he went into battle with the Maratha army, was always the standard of Savoy.

In Chambery there were no openings for the son of a shopkeeper. The government was bureaucratic, and all important posts were reserved for the Italian nobility. Young de Boigne's only amusement was fencing. He gave a great deal of time to the sport, and became a skilled fencer. At seventeen he fought a duel with a Sardinian noble, and ran him through the body. Benoit had to leave Savoy, changing his name to de Boigne.

His father, however, was well off and bought for Benoit an ensign's commission in the Clare Regiment of the Irish Brigade. Although mainly composed of Irish, the Brigade was open, as the Foreign Legion is today, to adventurers of all nations. But to get promotion one had to be Irish. Five years later de Boigne was still an ensign. In disgust he resigned his commission, and, obtaining a letter of introduction to Count Orloff, made his way to Russia.

Count Orloff was then dictator of Russia. He was the lover of the Empress Catherine II, whom he had placed on the throne after murdering her husband the Emperor Peter. But preoccupied with the cares of State, he could no longer satisfy the desires of the amorous Catherine; so he conceived the ingenious idea of substituting for himself a series of handsome and virile young men. De Boigne had youth, vigour and charm, and it did not take him long to find favour with the Empress; but, if Catherine was fond of good looking young men, she was still more fond of change. (The Begum Samru was of a similar disposition.) When she had had enough of de Boigne she gave him a captain's commission and sent him to fight the Turks in the Aegean. The young adventurer was taken prisoner at Tenedos and sold as a slave. He spent the next seven months drawing water from a well in Constantinople.

Ransomed by his father — who, it seems, never neglected his duty towards his son — de Boigne again presented himself to his bored Empress; and to get rid of him again she promoted him to the rank of major and sent him to explore Central Asia — a polite form of dismissal.

To Central Asia went de Boigne. Meeting some English merchants at Smyrna, full of travellers' tales about India, he resigned the Russian service and decided to try his luck in India. Arriving at Madras, he obtained an appointment as a sub-lieutenant in the Madras army; but he was a Frenchman, and his attentions to the wife of a fellow officer were misunderstood, and he had to resign. From Madras he went to Calcutta, with a letter of introduction to Warren Hastings, who, taking a liking to de Boigne, sent him to the Nawab of Oudh, who had already done so much for Claude Martine. The two Frenchmen met and became life-long friends. The Nawab gave de Boigne a letter of credit for twelve thousand rupees and a *khilat* which de Boigne sold for four thousand rupees; but soon afterwards a gang of robbers, instigated by Madhavrao Sindhia, who was curious to know more about the adventurer, stole his money and papers. De Boigne was once again a beggar; but this was the turning point in his fortunes.

Madhavrao Sindhia had studied the papers taken from de Boigne's baggage, and had been carefully watching the Savoyard's movements. He had learnt from fighting against the British and his loss of Gwalior the immense value of European discipline and tactics. When the Marathas had been routed by the Afghans at Panipat, and Sindhia had escaped with his life and a lame leg, the best fight had been put up by a corps of infantry trained on the European model. Unfortunately there had not been enough of these troops; and the Marathas' hit-and-run tactics, useful in skirmishes, were of no help in a pitched battle. But Sindhia, a shrewd man, learnt from experience. Now he offered de Boigne fifteen thousand rupees a month to raise two battalions of regular infantry, modelled as closely as possible on the East India Company's troops.

De Boigne's opportunity — and test — had come. It was no easy job with which he was faced. First he had to select officers, and he gathered around him a number of other adventurers,

French, Dutch and English: chief among them Perron, who was to be his less glorious successor, Robert Sutherland and James Skinner. Then he had to raise recruits. The Maratha army, except for cavalry, was to consist of very few Marathas; most of the soldiers were Rajputs, and Jats and Rohillas from the northern provinces.

De Boigne created an arsenal, a cannon foundry and a small-arms factory; and in five months he had under his command two excellent infantry battalions. He never went to bed before midnight and he rose before dawn. His working days were seven a week, his working hours eighteen a day.

The first time Sindhia inspected his new battalions, he was struck by their discipline. The Deccan soldiery had been till then an army of "irregular ruffians". Every trooper owned his own horse and arms. Unlike the Rajput who fought for his honour, these soldiers fought for money and plunder; naturally they had no wish to imperil their property. His horse and spear were his only capital, and rather than lose them he would often prefer flight in a dangerous situation.

De Boigne's battalions were soon tested. In 1785 the fugitive Emperor Shah Alam had called in the help of Madhavrao Sindhia, who, by re-seating the Emperor on the throne and using him as a figurehead, actually made himself master of the Moghul Empire. The rise of Sindhia roused the fury of the Moghul nobles and caused the Rajput princes to renounce their vassalage to the Empire. Sindhia, at the head of the Imperial Army and de Boigne's battalions, marched into Rajputana. He was attacked by a great Rathor force at Lalsot to the south-east of Jaipur. At the start of the battle the Moghul generals of the Imperial Army, Mohammed Beg and his nephew Ismail Beg, suddenly changed sides, taking their men over to the Rathors. Sindhia ordered an attack before any more troops could go over.

Ismail Beg's cavalry charged the Maratha horse and dispersed them without much difficulty. Immediately afterwards ten thousand mounted Rathors charged de Boigne's battalions, which were all that remained of Sindhia's left wing. De Boigne drew up his men in a hollow square with his guns inside, and waited until the splendid Rathor horsemen were within a hundred yards. Then he ordered his front rank to withdraw behind the guns; and as the Rathors charged home they were met with a terrific storm of grape shot. What was left of the Jodhpur cavalry reached the guns and sabred the artillerymen; but de Boigne ordered his infantry to fire point blank into the struggling mass. The Rathors broke and fled, but before they could reform de Boigne led a counter-attack. This completed the rout, and the Jodhpur horse galloped from the field.

Sindhia now ordered a general assault; but the Imperial forces were determined to fight no further for the Maratha chief. They marched across to the enemy with their drums beating and their colours flying, leaving Sindhia alone with his broken cavalry and de Boigne's two undefeated battalions.

Sindhia withdrew hastily and tried to retrieve his fortunes by allying himself with the Jats of Bharatpur. Their ruler had also engaged a Frenchman named Lestineaux to raise a body of disciplined infantry. At Chaksana the new allies met the Imperial Army commanded by Ismail Beg and a Rohilla named Ghulam Kadir, who was to become notorious in the next few months. A mass of Rajput cavalry charged the Maratha irregular horse and foot, and broke them; but they could make no impression on either Lestineaux's or de Boigne's battalions. These two retreated to Bharatpur: meanwhile Ismail Beg had taken Agra from its Maratha garrison, and Ghulam Kadir retreated with the plunder he had collected to his native Rohilkhand.

The astute Sindhia, seeing his enemies divided, resumed the offensive and marched to the relief of Agra. Ismail Beg charged de Boigne's and Lestineaux's battalions; but the sepoys stood their ground and shot down the charging horsemen. De Boigne ordered a general advance, stormed Ismail Beg's camp and scattered his army. Ismail Beg, twice wounded, swam his horse across the Jumna and fled to Ghulam Kadir's camp. The latter marched on Delhi, the gates of which were treacherously opened to him. The only person who attempted to oppose him was the Begum Samru, but her forces were inadequate and she had to retire. Ghulam Kadir seized the Emperor, gouged out his eyes through frustration at being unable to extract from him a treasure which in fact did not exist (Nadir Shah had seen to that), and extracted money and jewellery by torturing members of the Imperial family including the women. Ismail Beg was disgusted with his ally, and went back to Sindhia; and eventually a great Maratha force reoccupied Delhi, released the Emperor and executed Ghulam Kadir. Whatever treasure Ghulam Kadir had collected was removed by Lestineaux, who had been in charge of the pursuit. This unprincipled adventurer promptly disappeared with it, out of the country. Some twenty-five years later he turned up in Syria, a ragged, impoverished individual, sponging on the local Europeans. No trace was ever found of the Imperial jewels.

Shortly after the recapture of Delhi, de Boigne resigned from Sindhia's service. He had asked for an increase of ten battalions under his command, but Sindhia's Maratha officers were jealous of his success and persuaded Sindhia to refuse this request. At Lucknow, de Boigne joined Claude Martine in the cloth and indigo business; but Sindhia, finding himself in difficulties with an army whose morale had been affected by de Boigne's resignation, and worried by the growing power of his Maratha rival Tukoji Holkar, was soon asking de Boigne to return and raise ten battalions on his own terms.

De Boigne, a soldier at heart, could not resist the offer. Away flew ledgers and day books, receipts and bills of lading. Handing back the business to Claude Martine, he dashed to sacred Mathura, Sindhia's headquarters. There he took over his own two mutinous battalions, as well as Lestineaux's. The other seven battalions he recruited in Rohilkhand, Oudh and the valleys of the Jumna and Ganges. His salary was raised to ten thousand rupees, and he was assigned for the cost of his division the whole Doab — the Jumna-Ganges region — with Aligarh as his headquarters. This region's revenue was about £200,000 a year, but through good management de Boigne soon increased it to £300,000.

At that period there was no real administration in India, as this is understood today. The remains of Akbar's system had broken down. In the vast northern region known as Hindustan, stretching from Allahabad to Karnal and from the Vindhyas to the southern slopes of the Himalayas, society was completely paralysed, normal occupations at a standstill. The tramplings of Moghul and Maratha were not the only cause of this. Roads had ceased to exist, towns were deserted. Intercourse between neighbouring villages was made difficult by tigers and wild elephants. The demoralised farmers, not knowing who would reap their crops, reduced their labour to the lowest level necessary for the cultivation of food for themselves. And when the rains failed, production ceased altogether, and thousands died of starvation.

In the heart of this unhappy region de Boigne, backed by an appreciative Sindhia, attempted the first restoration of law and order. The civil administration had two departments: the Persian side, conducted by Indian writers and accountants; and the 'French' office under his own supervision. Public dues were fixed by a rough assessment of landed estates, and were collected punctually, thanks to the presence of the military. There were no courts and no system of law, but reports of enquiries by local officials were sent to the General, who gave the final decision, awarding punishments according to his own discretion. De Boigne was generally a safe arbitrator, and the poor preferred him to any other.

He rose, we are told by a young English officer, Thomas Twining, who visited him, at the crack of dawn; surveyed his stores and factories, inspected his troops, transacted the civil business of his division, gave audience, received the reports of his criminal and fiscal officers, and got through his correspondence, official and private. If today de Boigne is not remembered, it is due to the neglect of English historians, who busied themselves with epics of their own countrymen; but he was a legend in his own time, and had Sindhia lived, and de Boigne not returned to Europe, it is conceivable that the British would never have got a permanent foothold in northern India.

Fifty years after de Boigne left India, old men spoke with genuine regret for the passing of his administration. The introduction of British rule, with its sure, inflexible methods, had the effect of interrupting this welfare and producing a contrast. When land became a security for debt, and ancestral acres were brought to the hammer for defaults of government dues, it was not to be wondered at if people sighed for the days of Sindhia and de Boigne. Perhaps even now something can be learned from the records of de Boigne's administration.

On the twentieth of June 1790 the ten battalions received their "baptism of fire". Ismail Beg and the rajas of Jaipur and Jodhpur were once again in arms against Madhavrao Sindhia. De Boigne's division, flanked by Maratha cavalry, came out to meet them, and in a few hours de Boigne was able to write to a friend: "Thank God, I have realised all the sanguine expectations of Sindhia." The Rajput and Moghul cavalry were destroyed, a hundred cannon taken, and the town of Patan carried by storm. Ismail Beg, though as always in the forefront of the battle, managed to escape again when he saw that all was lost. Sindhia was all gratitude to de Boigne for this success; his only criticism being that de Boigne had returned to the vanquished the plunder taken by the Maratha soldiers.

The raja of Jodhpur would not accept the defeat as final. The Rathor women taunted him and his nobles with having lost the five things that a Rajput cherishes most — their horses, their shoes, their turbans, their moustaches and the "Sword of Marwar". The raja called out every Rathor capable of bearing arms, from the ages of sixteen to sixty, and in September they assembled at Merta, sworn to restore their honour or perish.

The rugged Arravallis had caught the first rays of the morning sun when de Boigne decided to take the offensive and attack the Rajput camp. The Rathor horsemen were clothed in saffron, which meant that they would neither give nor take quarter. "Remember Patan!" they cried, and, drunk with opium, repeatedly charged the squares of de Boigne. They were shot down in hundreds only to reform and charge again. It is said that four thousand saddles were emptied in the return ride. At last only fifteen were left. They dismounted and fought on foot until they too were killed.

By three in the afternoon de Boigne had taken the town of Merta. The grateful Sindhia showered honours on him. He ordered him to raise another ten thousand men at once, and three years later (1793) another ten thousand. De Boigne now had under his command a corps of thirty thousand men with a hundred and twenty guns.

It was the ambition of every soldier to serve under de Boigne. Half a century before his time, he had made innovations undreamt of in the armies of the Indian princes. From the beginning, one of his main objects was to minimise the horrors of war. Officers and soldiers who were wounded in his service received financial compensation; disabled men were awarded grants of land, and special provision was made for the relatives of those killed in action. A medical department, attached to which was an ambulance corps, was on hand at every battle. Medical aid to the wounded is taken for granted today. It was unheard of in India until the end of the eighteenth century. Conditions under de Boigne were in fact better than in the Company's army.

He was a born leader of men. "There was something in his face and bearing," wrote the *Bengal Journal* in 1790, "that depicted the hero, and compelled implicit obedience. In deportment he was commanding, and walked with the majestic tread of conscious greatness. The strong cast of his countenance and the piercing expression of his eyes indicated the force and power of his mind. On the grand stage, where he acted so brilliant and important a part for ten years, he was at once dreaded and idolised, feared and admired, respected and beloved".

De Boigne's successes led Tukoji Holkar to raise another disciplined force, under the command of a Breton called du Drenec. When the rival Maratha armies met at Laikhari in September 1793, du Drenec's men were outnumbered; and, although they fought well, they were cut to pieces. This victory made Madhavrao Sindhia the greatest ruler in India. But just as it seemed possible that his scheme for a confederation of Indian States might come to pass, he fell victim to a fever and died near Poona. Power in India had always been the prerogative of individuals, and with Sindhia's passing a whole Empire was to pass out of existence.

Colonel Malleson, in his *Final French Struggles*, wrote: "It must never be lost sight of that the great dream of Madhavrao Sindhia's life was to unite all the native powers of India in one great confederacy against the English. In this respect he was the most far-sighted statesman that India has ever produced. . . . It was a grand idea, capable of realisation by Madhavji, but by him alone, and which, but for his death, would have been realised."

A change of masters is rarely welcome; and Daulat Rao did not have the attractive character of his predecessor Madhavrao. De Boigne began to think of returning to his homeland. He had not rested for eighteen years, and his health was beginning to show signs of the strain. He resigned his service, but Daulat Rao could not be induced to accept his resignation until December 1795.

On the plains of Agra, where seven years before he had won an Empire for Madhavrao Sindhia, de Boigne paraded his battalions in review for the last time. Here is the scene as conjured up by Herbert Compton: "The General, tall, gaunt and martial, his rugged features showing signs of failing health, is seated on his charger. He watches with sadness in his piercing eyes his veterans passing before him for the last time. The sword, that has so often led the way to victory, now, and for the last time, trembles in his hand as he brings it to the salute."

Four years after de Boigne left India, Sindhia's successor wrote to him: "Since it has pleased the Universal Physician to restore to you the blessing of health, and having regard to our jealous impatience to see you again, it is your bounden duty no more to prolong your stay in Europe, but to appear before the presence with all possible despatch . . . without your wisdom the execution of the greatest of projects is entirely suspended."

But de Boigne never returned, and his successor Perron, like the great Sindhia's successor, was not equal to the challenge of the British.

When de Boigne reached England in 1797, carrying with him a fortune of £400,000, he was forty-seven years old. With him were his Persian wife, whom we know only by the name of "Helene", and his two children, Banoo and Ali Baksh. Little Ali Baksh was baptized Charles Alexander Benet de Boigne in London, and was destined to inherit de Boigne's fortune and estates at Chambery in Savoy. Unfortunately for de Boigne he went early in 1799 to a charity concert in London. There he heard a girl of seventeen sing beautifully, and the song and the fresh charm and beauty of the girl turned his head. The man who had conquered half of India became the singer's slave. She was a Mlle. Osmond, the daughter of a French nobleman who had fled to England during the French Revolution.

A few days after the concert the General asked for the hand of Mlle. Osmond. She was very frank. She did not, could not love a man so much older than herself; but, as her family were ruined, she would marry the General to assure their comfort. De Boigne accepted her conditions. In 1804 he took his wife to Paris and persuaded Buonaparte to allow her parents to return to France. Then he went home to Savoy and bought the castle of Buisson Rond, close to Chambery.

As expected, the couple did not get on well together. Mlle. Osmond felt that their union should not descend to a physical level. Leaving her husband at Chambery, she went to stay in Paris, where she lived lavishly on her husband's money.

De Boigne, alone at Chambery, turned his attention to his

native town. He spent £120,000 in building poor houses, schools, hospitals and orphanages, and erected the first properly managed lunatic asylum in Europe. His chief pleasures were visits from Englishmen or Frenchmen he had known in India. Both Colonel Tod, the author of *Annals of Rajasthan*, and Grant Duff, the historian of the Marathas, have written of the cordiality and kindness shown to them when they visited de Boigne at Buisson Rond. His only companion at that time was an old servant he had brought with him from India and who managed all the household arrangements.

This was de Boigne two years before his death: "His frame and stature were Herculean, and he was full six feet two inches in height. His aspect was mild and unassuming, and he was unostentatious in his habit and demeanour, preserving at his advanced age all the gallantry and politeness of the *vielle cour*. He disliked, from modesty, to refer to his past deeds, and so seemed to strangers to have lost his memory. But in the society of those who could partake of the emotions it awakened, the name of Merta always stirred in him associations whose call he could not resist. The blood would mount to his temples, and the old fire came into his eyes, as he recalled, with inconceivable rapidity and eloquence, the story of that glorious day. But he spoke of himself as if it were another, and always concluded with the words, 'My past appears a dream!' "

On the twenty-first of June 1830 the old adventurer passed away amid the deep and sincere grief of Chambery. Citizens flocked to his funeral. For three days the shops were closed. The King of Sardinia had a bust of de Boigne placed in the public library; and from money raised by public subscription, a fountain flanked by elephants and surmounted by the General's statue was placed in the public square. The modern tourist, hurrying through Chambery, must often wonder what this exotic fountain is all about; few stop to enquire.

But the name of de Boigne is still honoured in Savoy, the de Boigne fountain still plays in Chambery Square, and the descendants of Sindhia's French General and his Persian lady still live in the castle of Buisson Rond.

THE ROMANCE OF THE MAIL RUNNER

WE FIND LITTLE that is romantic in the post office today; but there was a time, over a hundred years ago, when the carrying of the mails was a hazardous venture, and the mail runner, or *hirkara* as he was called, had to be armed with a sword or spear. That was before the railways and the air services made the delivery of the mail a routine affair.

Though the first public postal service was introduced in India by Warren Hastings in 1774, the Kings and Emperors of India had always maintained their own personal postal system. Their rule was effective partly due to their excellent means of communication, by which despatches were passed on from hand to hand either by runner or horseman. When Ibn Batuta was travelling in India in the middle of the fourteenth century he found an organised system of couriers established throughout the country by Mohammed Bin Tughlak.

"There is a foot-courier at a distance of every mile," wrote lbn Batuta, "and at every three miles there is an inhabited village, and outside it three sentry boxes where the couriers sit prepared for motion with their loins girded. In the hands of each is a whip about two cubits long, and upon the head of this are small bells. Whenever one of the couriers leaves any city, he takes his despatches in one hand and the whip, which he keeps constantly shaking, in the other. In this manner he proceeds to the nearest foot-courier and, as he approaches, shakes his whip. Upon this out comes another who takes the despatches and so proceeds to the next. It is for this reason that the Sultan receives his despatches in so short a time."

This system was of course established for the convenience of the Emperor, and was continued with various innovations by successive Moghul Emperors. In the eighteenth century the East India Company established a postal system of its own to facilitate the conveyance of letters between different factories; but it was only during Warren Hastings' administration that a Postmaster-General was appointed, and the general public could avail of the service, paying a fee on their letters.

Letters were then carried in leather wallets on the backs of runners, who were changed at stages of eight miles. At night the runners were accompanied by torch-bearers — in wilder parts, by drummers called *dug-dugi-wallas* — to frighten away wild animals.

In places where tigers were known to be active, mail runners were armed with bows and arrows; but these were seldom effective, and the mail carrier often fell victim to a man-eating tiger. In the Hazaribagh district (through which the mail had to be carried on its way from Calcutta to Allahabad) there appears to have been a concentration of man-eating tigers.

There were four passes through this district, and the tigers had them well covered. We are told that "day after day, for nearly a fortnight, some of the mail runners were carried off."

Postal runners were largely drawn from the tribal races, many of whom were animist by religion. They were ready to face wild beasts and wandering criminals, but would go miles to avoid an evil spirit in a tree.

Mail robberies were frequent, and in 1808 the mail between Kanpur and Fatehgarh was looted once a week on an average. The mail runner had to be fleet of foot, not only for the purpose of delivering the mail speedily, but also for outpacing any dacoits he might encounter on the road. Twelve rupees a month was the runner's salary, not very much even in those years. His courage and honesty were, therefore, qualities to be admired. Seldom did a runner abscond with a mail-bag, though it nearly always contained valuables and registered articles.

In 1822 horsemen were substituted for mail runners, but they proved uneconomical, because it meant feeding both horses and men. More surprising, horses took twelve days from Calcutta to Meerut, compared to ten days taken by runners, who covered the distance in shorter stages. Eventually the *dak-ghari* — the equivalent of the English "coach and pair" — was introduced, and gradually established itself. Runners were, of course, still used, because the coach could only keep to the principal highways.

After Younghusband's expedition to Tibet in 1904, the British established a postal system between India and Lhasa, through Sikkim.

The mail runners — in this case drawn from Indo-Tibetan border tribes — faced snow-covered passes, swift rivers which could be crossed only in yak-skin canoes or on crude ropeways, Himalayan bears and snow-leopards, and perhaps even Abominable Snowmen!

The mails were first carried by train in 1855 when the East Indian Railway was opened between Calcutta and Raniganj, a distance of 122 miles. Today, the principal cities of India are connected by fast air mail services.

But even now, in remote parts of the country, in isolated hill areas where there are no roads, the mail is carried on foot, the postman often covering five to six miles every day.

He never runs, true, and he might occasionally stop at a village to share a hookah with a friend, but he is a reminder of those early pioneers of the postal system, the mail runners of India.

ZOFFANY'S *LAST SUPPER*

IN THE YEAR 1787, when St. John's Church in Calcutta was nearing completion, the Royal Academician John Zoffany presented the church with a painting of *The Last Supper* which he had completed in Calcutta that year. The story of this painting and Zoffany's own career makes interesting reading for those who like digging into the history of minor but colourful figures of the past.

John Zoffany was one of the earliest Royal Academicians. It was said that he was obliged to leave England due to the ill-feeling he had roused because of his indulgence in the habit of introducing the likenesses of his friends and acquaintances into his paintings without their permission, very often presenting them in an unflattering light. Arriving in India in 1781, he went first to Lucknow, where an eccentric Nawab appreciated people like Zoffany. He was made Court Painter, and in a few years amassed a fortune by painting the portraits of members of the Nawab's family and retinue. One of his subjects was Claude Martine, military adventurer, trader, money-lender to the Nawabs and, through his last will and testament, public benefactor. The two were great friends, and Zoffany did some attractive portraits of Martine, his mistress and his friends.

In 1787 Zoffany was residing in Calcutta. His name is found in an almanac of that year, under the profession "Artist and Portrait Painter". *The Calcutta Gazette* of 12 April 1787 announced: "We hear that Mr. Zoffany is employed in painting a large historical picture, 'The Last Supper': he has already made considerable progress in the work, which promises to equal any production which has yet appeared from the brush of this able artist; and, with that spirit of liberality for which he has ever been distinguished, we understand he means to present it to the public as an altar-piece for the new church."

The church accepted the gift, and were anxious to compensate the artist, but had no funds left at their disposal. Instead, they sent him an enthusiastic letter of thanks. When the church was consecrated and the painting hung in its place, the latter caused quite a sensation in Calcutta society. It was found that the figures in the picture were more or less faithful likenesses of members of the community. The three principal figures in the picture, Jesus, St. John, and Judas Iscariot, were easily recognizable. The original for Jesus was a Greek priest, Father Porthenio, who was well-known in Calcutta for his good works. St. John was represented by Mr. Blaquiere, a well-known magistrate; and Judas Iscariot was recognized as an old resident of Calcutta, Tulloh, the auctioneer. The names of those who were models for the other disciples have not come down to us.

Calcutta society was scandalised by Zoffany's sense of humour but he was not disconcerted; and when, some years later, he was asked to paint an altar-piece for a church at Brentford in England, he did the same thing. Again it was a picture of the Last Supper, and again he took his friends and neighbours for models.

Both pictures can still be seen — one in St. George's Church at Brentford, the other in St. John's, Calcutta. "The painting is there," writes a friend from Calcutta, "over the left side of the altar, perhaps 8 ft. by 8 ft., framed in gilt; in the foreground is Judas, looking like Alan Hale,* except that Hale never played villains, and this chap has his face turned away from the group and has a very guilty expression. He also has curly red hair and a curly red beard. Nearly all the painters from early Italians downwards have given Judas red hair. Sometimes it's curly, sometimes it's straight, but it's almost always red."

Zoffany is still considered an able portrait painter. And he has one distinction. On the voyage home to England, his ship was wrecked on a lonely island. To avoid starvation the survivors, Zoffany among them, cast lots, and a young seaman was duly eaten. Thus, Zoffany was the first and, it is hoped, the last Royal Academician to become a cannibal.

---

* A star of the early talkies.

CLAUDE MARTINE: A FRENCHMAN AT THE COURT OF OUDH

STILL ONE OF THE MORE conspicuous landmarks in Lucknow — capital of the Indian Union's Uttar Pradesh State, and formerly chief city of the fabulous kings of Oudh — is the building of the Martiniere School: a strange edifice, a palace that is a mixture of Gothic and Moghul architecture. When its builder and owner, Major-General Claude Martine, died at Lucknow in 1800, he bequeathed it as a school "for the instruction of the English language and religion"; and the story of Constantia, as the palace was named, is the story of an unusual adventurer, a businessman who became a Major-General without seeing a major battle.

Martine was a Frenchman. Born at Lyons in 1732, his father expected that he would follow the family business, manufacturing silk, but the boy had other ambitions, and plans of his own. He ran away from home when he was fifteen and still at school, and enlisted in the French army. In 1757, the year of Plassey, the Count de Lally was appointed French Governor of Pondicherry, and Martine, who had always dreamt of sailing to India, volunteered for the Count's bodyguard. He was taken on without many questions being asked. The bodyguard consisted of deserters, military criminals and other choice rascals; but it went to India, bringing Martine to Pondicherry in 1758.

Lally was a severe, almost tyrannical disciplinarian, unpopular with his men; and when the British laid siege to Pondicherry, the bodyguard with Martine in tow deserted and went over to the English. Martine returned with the British troops to Madras, where — something of the opportunist — he volunteered to raise a corps of French cavalry from among the prisoners, to serve under the British. His offer was accepted, and he was commissioned as an ensign.

Shortly after Martine had formed his corps, he was ordered to Bengal. The journey had to be made by sea, up the Bay of Bengal. During the voyage the ship sprang a leak, and he and his men were lucky to get away in boats and land safely at

Calcutta.

In Calcutta, in the middle of the eighteenth century, it was necessary to enter "society" if an officer wished to advance his prospects. This Martine did with zest. Wining and dining was then practised as an art, and the young Frenchman soon made himself at home with the cream of Calcutta's English society, especially its women. One of them, Mrs. Fay, has left us an amusing account of a Calcutta dinner of that time:

"We were frequently told in England," she wrote home, "that the heat in Bengal destroyed the appetite. I must own that I never yet saw any proof of that: on the contrary, I cannot help thinking that I never saw an equal quantity of victuals consumed. We dine, too, at two o'clock, in the very heat of the day. At this moment Mr. F. is looking out with a hawk's eye for his dinner, and, though still much of an invalid, I have no doubt of being able to pick a bit myself. I will give you our bill of fare, and the general prices of things: a soup, a roast fowl, curry and rice, a mutton pie, a forequarter of lamb, a rice pudding, tarts, very good cheese, fresh churned butter, fine bread, excellent Madeira (that is expensive, but eatables are very cheap). A whole sheep costs but two rupees, a lamb one rupee, six good fowls or ducks ditto, twelve pigeons ditto, and twelve pounds of bread ditto."

In due course Martine became a captain, but in 1764 his corps was disbanded, as his men — most of them professional deserters — had mutinied. Martine, however, was popular with the English. Finding that he was a good draughtsman, they sent him as a surveyor to the north-eastern districts of Bengal; then to the province of Oudh, still an independent kingdom, though under the influence of the East India Company. Its annexation in 1856 was to be one of the causes of the 1857 uprising.

From the time he arrived at Lucknow, capital of Oudh, Martine never had to look back. His life, till then, had been eventful: now it became profitable.

It was not long before his talents came to the notice of the Nawab, Asaf-ud-daula, a bulky, benevolent-looking despot with long walrus moustaches, who was attracted to anyone with unusual tastes or accomplishments. The fact that Martine "manufactured the first balloons that ever floated in the air of Asia" was sufficient recommendation for him. The Nawab was fascinated by balloons. Once, as punishment to a barber (one of the fifty personal barbers) who had nicked him, he attached the unfortunate man to one of the balloons with which Martine was experimenting. "Borne rapidly aloft and carried off at a great pace across country", the barber landed safely on an Englishman's property, but took to his heels and was never seen again.

If fifty personal barbers should be considered superfluous, what can be said for the four thousand gardeners who looked after the palace gardens, and the several hundred cooks in the royal kitchens? The Nawab was also a man of sporting tastes: he kept a thousand dogs trained for hunting, and 300,000 fighting cocks and pigeons. One of his favourite sports, introduced by a certain Colonel Mordaunt, was the racing of old women in sacks. The Nawab said he had never found anything so enjoyable.

Asaf-ud-daula was considered benevolent for his time, and there was a verse about him that went:

To whom Heaven does not give
Asaf-ud-daula will.

He was certainly liberal with the money extracted from his subjects who, thanks to the rapacity of the Nawab's revenue collectors, were in a miserable condition.

One of the recipients of the Nawab's generosity was Claude Martine. Apart from his ability with balloons, Martine was also a skilled gunner, and this gave Asaf-ud-daula a more solid reason for requesting the Bengal government for the Frenchman's services. Calcutta approving, Martine was appointed superintendent of the Nawab's arsenal and artillery.

It was not long before he became confidential adviser to the Nawab and, during the next twenty years, he was often the chief negotiator between the king and the Company. It says something for his diplomacy that throughout this period he retained the trust and confidence of both the Nawab and the English, neither of whom trusted each other. And again it says something for his shrewd opportunism that in these twenty years he was able to amass a fortune amounting to nearly half a million sterling.

How did he make his money?

Judicious investments in the indigo and saltpetre industries was one method. Vast fortunes were made by the indigo planters until the manufacture of synthetic dyes killed the industry. But apart from this, Martine was the "recognized channel" for petitions from all who desired any favour from the government, and in this capacity enormous bribes and presents of great value found their way into his hands. He educated the Nawab into an appreciation of the products of Europe, and then acted as his agent in procuring them. Finally his position at court was esteemed so secure that, in a country distracted by war and internal troubles, he soon became a sort of "safe deposit" for the valuables of the Nawab's subjects, charging a commission of 12 per cent for the custody of articles committed to his care.

It is not surprising that Martine acquired an immense fortune during his long stay in Lucknow. He was helped in this by his beautiful Persian mistress, "Lise" as he called her, who, having access to the royal harem, also had access to much of the palace intrigue. But Martine was considered honest according to the standards of his time, which were very different to present-day standards. He would have been considered a fool not to take commission on everything he supplied, when everyone else did so. And what he did supply — tapestries, pictures, chandeliers from Europe — were the best that could be bought. Due to his efforts, the Royal Academician, John Zoffany, was appointed Court Painter to the Nawab, and during his stay in India painted many valuable portraits of various Indian rulers and their families.

One of Martine's closest friends — though they met only occasionally — was General de Boigne, the French adventurer who had trained Madhavji Sindhia's Maratha army, and had done much to make Sindhia master of most of northern India. Martine helped de Boigne to make some useful investments. De Boigne returned to Europe with his wealth, where a disastrous marriage spoilt his enjoyment of it; but Martine never seriously considered leaving India.

Though wealthier than most generals, one of Martine's principal ambitions was to achieve a high rank in the British Army; and in 1790 he was able to have his wish fulfilled, through a clever move on his own part. War had broken out in the South between the British and Tippu Sultan and as his contribution to it Martine presented the Company with a number of fine horses, sufficient for a cavalry regiment. For this, he was made a colonel. Six years later he became a major-general. He was still on a captain's pay, but obviously this did not worry him. Prestige appears to have mattered a great deal then, as it does today.

Perhaps the most remarkable achievement of Claude Martine was the building of his house, Constantia, now the Martiniere school. It was a castle, built on the banks of the river Gomti "on scientific and hygienic principles" as they would say today. It contained a series of flats adapted to cope with the varying temperatures of Lucknow, which knows extremes of heat and cold. In the hot weather Martine lived in a subterranean suite, cool and sheltered from the fierce glare of the sun. During the monsoon he ascended to the upper storey, as the underground chambers and often the ground floor would be flooded by the swollen Gomti. (Lucknow's worst floods in 1960 touched the 8-foot mark on Constantia's walls, and the boys had to be evacuated in boats.) During the cold weather, Martine remained on the ground floor.

When Warren Hastings, as Governor-General, visited Lucknow in 1814, he wrote this of Constantia:

"The house, built in the English style, stands upon a gentle elevation with some extent of lawn about it. The idea of it was probably taken from those castles of pastry which used to adorn desserts in former days. . . . The doors of the principal floor were plated with iron, and each window was protected by an iron grate. Loopholes from passages above gave the means of firing in perfect security upon any persons who should force their way into these lower apartments. The spiral stone staircases were blocked at intervals with iron doors; in short, the whole was framed for protracted and desperate resistance. The parapets and pinnacles were decorated with a profusion of plaster lions, Grecian gods, and Chinese figures, forming the most whimsical assemblage imaginable. Still, the magnitude of the buildings, with its cupolas and spires, gave it a certain magnificence."

As the building has changed little in the past 150 years, a modern aesthete or architect would probably be more critical in his description of Constantia than was Warren Hastings. But Lucknow was never noted for its architecture. It was, and is, noted for its charm; and Constantia is very much a part of Lucknow's charm.

During the last fifteen years of his life Martine suffered considerably from a stone in the bladder. He cured himself temporarily, but the disease recurred, and he died in 1800, at the age of sixty-two.

Earlier that year he had drawn up his will, which was a fascinating document. It contained over forty clauses, and began by "acknowledging with penitence that self-interest has been my guiding principle throughout life." After providing for Lise, he left his entire fortune in the form of charitable legacies. Amongst them were three for the poor of Calcutta, Chandernagore and Lucknow, the interest from which was to be given to the poor at regular intervals. To this day it is still done at Lucknow.

He left a large sum in trust to the Government of Bengal for the establishment of the Martiniere school in Constantia, and for schools at Calcutta and his native Lyons, with special provisions for children from needy families. Knowing that the Nawab envied his house and wished to buy it, Martine stipulated that he should be buried in the basement floor, thus desecrating the place in the eyes of the Nawab: no Mohammedan may inhabit a tomb.

"When I am dead," went this remarkable clause in Martine's will, "I request that my body may be salted, put in spirits, or embalmed, and afterwards deposited in a leaden coffin made of some sheet lead in my godown, which is to be put in another of sissoo wood, and then deposited in the cave in the small round room north-east in Constantia, with two feet of masonry raised above it, which is to bear the following inscription:

Major-General Claude Martine,
Born at Lyons, January 1738,
Arrived in India as a common soldier, and died
(at Lucknow, the 13th September 1800) a major-general;
and he is buried in this tomb.
Pray for his soul.

When Lady Fanny Parkes visited his tomb in 1831 she mentioned that a bust of the general adorned the vault, that lights were constantly burnt before the tomb, and that it was guarded by four life-size plaster sepoys, with arms reversed, placed in the four corners of the room.

The plaster sepoys have long since gone. Probably they were

destroyed when, in 1857, real sepoys occupied and ransacked Constantia, destroying Martine's tomb, and scattering his bones about the vault. Later the bones were recovered, and the tomb and inscription restored. Fortunately the plaster soldiers could not be restored, for they were samples of Martine's sometimes dubious artistic taste. A lover of the ostentatious, Martine did occasionally show good taste, and at his death his library contained more than 4000 books in Latin, Italian, French, English, Persian and Sanskrit, and he left a collection of a hundred and fifty oil paintings, amongst them forty-seven paintings and sketches by Zoffany and a complete set of Daniell's views of India. A private soldier without any formal schooling, he died a general and a patron of the arts. No other adventurer managed to be both!

It is by the Martiniere school that Martine is best remembered today. If it were not for his charitable legacies, his name would have been forgotten along with those of other minor soldiers of fortune, for he did not distinguish himself as a soldier or statesman; but he was an adventurer of another sort — an enterprising speculator, and one of the few Europeans who were able to adapt themselves happily to an Indian way of life without completely cutting themselves off from the customs and comforts of their homeland.

Today, most of the boys at the Martiniere are Indian; many have European forbears. At a dinner on the anniversary of Martine's death they still drink a toast to "The Memory of the Founder".

THE STORY OF A HILL STATION

VISITORS TO Mussoorie frequently find themselves persuaded to climb to the top of a local peak called "Gun Hill", from which they are able to enjoy a view of both the plains and the Greater Himalayas. They will also see the Mussoorie waterworks; but of a "gun" there is no sign, and they may be pardoned for wondering how the hill acquired its impressive name. The writer hopes to enlighten them on this, and other aspects, of the hill station's distant though not ancient past.

Before 1919, the Mussoorie public used to be told the time at noon by the firing of a gun from the peak known as "Gun Hill". Perhaps guns were cheaper than clocks in those days; I cannot think of any other sound reason for the system. It was not very popular with the local residents. At first the gun faced east, but soon after its installation (shortly after 1857), Miss Bryan of "Grey Castle Nursing Home," and then Miss Hamilton of the same institution, complained that when the gun was fired "it often loosed plaster from the ceiling of the wards, which fell on patients' beds and unnerved them". It could not be pointed north, because it would then have blasted away Mr. Yerborough's house, "Dilkusha"; so it was faced north-east, and almost immediately came a complaint from "Crystal Bank". Turned to the south, it almost succeeded in fulfilling its legitimate duty: the gunner forgot to remove the ramrod from the barrel; on booming noon to the populace, the cannon sent the ramrod clean through the roof of "Stella Cottage".

Public opinion was now mounting against the gun, and it was turned around once more — to face the Mall. Its boom was usually produced by ramming down the barrel a mixture of moist grass and cotton waste, after the powder was in place. Due to an accidental overcharge of powder, one of these cannonballs landed with some force in the lap of a lady who was being taken by *dandy* down to the plains. It was the last straw — or, to be exact, the last straw cannon-ball — for the gun was dismantled soon after this incident.

A peep into the life of a hill station before the turn of the century provides us with much interesting matter on European social life during that period. But before giving the reader further anecdotes, I should fill in the background with a brief historical sketch of Mussoorie.

In the year 1825, the "Superintendent of the Doon" was a certain Mr. F. J. Shore who found time from his official duties to scramble up to the hills then known as "Mansuri" because of the prevalence of a shrub known in the vernacular as the Mansur plant. He found that these hills had a number of flat areas, some of which accommodated the huts of cowherds who grazed their cattle on them during the summer months. Game was then plentiful in the hills, and the first construction was a shooting-box built jointly by Mr. Shore and Captain Young of the Sirmur Rifles. The first home, still recognizable, was "Mullingar" on Landour hill, built in 1826 by Captain Young. Soon Landour became a convalescent depot for British troops, and settlers began flocking to Mussoorie, building houses as far apart as "Cloud End" in the west and "Dahlia Bank" in the east, separated by a distance of some twelve miles. In 1832, Colonel Everest (after whom the mountain is named) as Surveyor-General opened his Survey of India office in "The Park" and made a road to it. Mussoorie is the original home of the department.

People came to Mussoorie for both business and pleasure, and amongst the pleasure-seekers we find the Hon'ble Emily Eden, sister of Lord George Eden, Earl of Auckland, Governor-General of India. In her journals she records that "in the afternoon we took a beautiful ride up to Landour, but the paths are much narrower on that side, and our courage somehow oozed out, and first we came to a place where they said, 'This was where poor Major Blundell and his pony fell over, and they were both dashed to atoms' — and then there was a board stuck in a tree, 'From this spot a private in the Cameroons fell and was killed'. . . . We had to get off our ponies and lead them, and altogether I thought much of poor Major Blundell! But it is impossible to imagine more beautiful scenery."

Though there were no proper roads in Mussoorie in those pioneer days, it is probably safe to assume that a number of cliff-edge accidents were caused by the beer that was then so cheap and plentiful in the hill station.

Mr. Bohle, one of the pioneers of brewing in India, started the

"Old Brewery" at Mussoorie in 1830. Two years later he got into trouble for supplying beer to soldiers who were alleged to have presented forged passes. Mr. Bohle was called to account by former Captain, now Colonel Young, for distilling spirits without a licence, and had to close his concern. But he was back in 1834, building "Bohle's Brewery".

However, the big push in the brewery business really began in 1876, when everyone suddenly acclaimed a much improved brew. The source was traced to Vat 42 in Whymper and Company's "Crown Brewery". The beer was re-tasted and re-tested until the diminishing level of the barrel revealed the perfectly brewed remains of a human being! Someone, probably drunk, had fallen into the beer barrel and been drowned, and, all unknown to himself, had given the beer trade a real fillip. Apocryphal though this story may sound, I have it on the authority of *A Mussoorie Miscellany*, its author going on to say that "meat was thereafter recognised as the missing component and as scrupulously added till more modern, and less cannibalistic, means were discovered to satiate the froth-blower".

A bold, bad place was Mussoorie in those days, according to the correspondent of *The Statesman* who, in his paper of twenty-second October 1884, wrote: "Ladies and gentlemen, after attending church, proceeded to a drinking shop, a restaurant adjoining the Library, and there indulged freely in *pegs*, not one but many; and at a Fancy Bazar held this season, a lady stood up on her chair and offered her kisses to gentlemen at Rs 5 each. What would they think of such a state of society at Home?"

Fortunately a *Statesman* correspondent was not present at a 1932 benefit show, when a Mussoorie lady stood up and auctioned a single kiss, for which a gentleman paid Rs 300!

In spite of these goings-on, or perhaps because of them, the inhabitants were conscious of their spiritual needs, and a number of churches were soon dotted about the hill station. The oldest of these is Christ Church (1836) whose chaplain almost a hundred years later was the fairminded Reverend T. W. Chisolm. In his usual Sunday service prayers in the year 1933, he sought God's help for Pandit Motilal Nehru, who was then seriously ill. There was an immediate storm in all official tea-cups and the chaplain was reprimanded. This caused one local writer of the time to comment, "that in these years of our Lord, Holy Orders can be interpreted to mean wholly Government orders."

Another public-spirited Mussoorie citizen was Captain A. W. Hearsey (a member of the famous Hearsey family, which had once owned large areas of the Dun). He was one of the first Anglo-Indian members of the Indian Congress. He had spoken at an All-India Congress Session, and a certain English language newspaper, in its report of the proceedings, referred to him as "a brown man who called himself a military captain." Without any delay, Captain Hearsey armed himself with a horse-whip, made a long train journey, and descended on the offices of the newspaper. On finding that the reporter in question was away on furlough, he said the editor would suit his purpose equally, and bursting into the editor's office, proceeded to horse-whip him. The litigation that followed evoked widespread interest at the time.

It is easy enough to get to Mussoorie today, but how did they manage it before the advent of the railway and the automobile? Of course, Mr. Shore and Captain Young merely scrambled up the goat tracks to get there; and Lady Eden used her pony to canter along paths and "up precipices"; but in the good old, *old* days (before the turn of the century), one detrained at Ghaziabad (some one hundred and fifty miles from one's destination), engaged a village bullock-cart, and proceeded in the direction of the Siwaliks as fast as only a bullock-cart can go. After that, one either walked, rode a pony, or was carried uphill in a doolie.

Later, the bullock-cart gave way to the *dak-ghari* and the tonga, and soon after the opening of the Hardwar-Dehra railway in 1901, the tonga was ousted by the motor car and the bus. Up to that time, the main overnight stop was at Rajpur, not Dehra, and the hostelries and forwarding agencies at Rajpur were the "Ellenborough Hotel", the "Prince of Wales Hotel", and the "Agency Retiring Rooms of Messrs. Buckle and Company's Bullock Train Agency". All are now in ruins.

There have been very few changes in Mussoorie during the last twenty years. Prices and taxes have gone up, but they have done so everywhere. The houses are still the same, many of them built in the last century. Some have been kept up quite well, others are in ruin. Rickshaws still ply on the Mall, and coolies still carry heavy loads up and down steep paths. There are more hotels (mostly for the middle-classes) and fewer boarding-houses. There are more schools. There are more restaurants. There is, in fact, more of nearly everything, except beer. At Rs 5 a bottle, Mussoorie's beer-drinking days are all but over.

The only edifices in the vicinity of this hill station that might pass muster as "ancient monuments" are the impressive ruins of the old breweries. They have all fallen down: sad reminders of the gay days when beer was less than a rupee a bottle, and only kisses were expensive.

A HILL STATION'S VINTAGE MURDERS

THERE IS LESS CRIME in the hills than in the plains, and so the few murders that do take place from time to time stand out as landmarks in the annals of a hill station.

Among the gravestones in the Mussoorie cemetery there is one which bears the inscription: "Murdered by the hand he befriended." This is the grave of Mr. James Reginald Clapp, a chemist's assistant, who was brutally done to death on the night of thirty-first August 1909.

Miss Ripley-Bean, who has spent most of her eighty-seven years in this hill station, remembers the case clearly, though she was only a girl at the time. From the details she has given me, and from a brief account in *A Mussoorie Miscellany*, now out of print, I am able to reconstruct this interesting case and of a couple of others which were the sensations of their respective "seasons".

Mr. Clapp was an assistant in the chemist's shop of Messrs. J.B. & E. Samuel (no longer in existence), situated in one of the busiest sections of the Mall. At that time the adjoining cantonment of Landour was an important convalescent centre for British soldiers. Mr. Clapp was popular with the soldiers, and he had befriended some of them when they had run short of money. He was a steady worker and sent most of his savings home, to his mother in Birmingham; she was planning to use the money to buy the house in which she lived.

At the time of the murder, Clapp was particularly friendly with a Corporal Allen, who was eventually to be hanged at the Naini Jail. The murder was brutal, the initial attack being launched with a soda-water bottle on the victim's head. Clapp's throat was then cut from ear to ear with his own razor, which was left behind in the room. The body was discovered on the floor of the shop the next morning by the proprietor, Mr. Samuel, who did not live on the premises.

Suspicion immediately fell on Corporal Allen because he had left Mussoorie that same night, arriving at Rajpur, in the foothills (a seven-mile walk by the bridle-path) many hours later than he was expected at a Rajpur boarding-house. According to some, Clapp had last been seen in the corporal's company.

There was other circumstantial evidence pointing to Allen's guilt. On the day of the murder, Mr. Clapp had received his salary, and this sum, in sovereigns and notes, was never traced. Allen was alleged to have made a payment in sovereigns at Rajpur. Someone had given Allen a biscuit-tin packed with sandwiches for his journey down, and it was thought that perhaps the tin had been used by the murderer as a safe for the money. But no tin was found, and Allen denied having had one with him.

Allen was arrested at Rajpur and brought back to Mussoorie under escort. He was taken immediately to the victim's bedside, where the body still lay, the police hoping that he might confess his guilt when confronted with the body of the victim; but Allen was unmoved, and protested his innocence.

Meanwhile, other soldiers from among Mr. Clapp's friends had collected on the Mall. They had removed their belts and were ready to lynch Allen as soon as he was brought out of the shop. The situation was tense, but further mishap was averted by the resourcefulness of Mr. Rust, a photographer, who, being of the same build as the corporal, put on an Army coat with a turned-up collar, and arranged to be handcuffed between two policemen. He remained with them inside the shop, in partial view of the mob, while the rest of the police party escorted the corporal out by a back entrance. Mr. Rust did not abandon his disguise or leave the shop until word arrived that Allen was secure in the police station.

Corporal Allen was eventually found guilty, and was hanged. But there were many who felt that he had never really been proved guilty, and that he had been convicted on purely circumstantial evidence; and looking back on the case from this distance in time one cannot help feeling that the soldier may have been a victim of circumstances, and perhaps of local prejudice, for he was not liked by his fellows. Allen himself hinted that he was not in the vicinity of the crime that night but in the company of a lady whose integrity he was determined to shield. If this was true, it was a pity that the lady prized her virtue more than her friend's life, for she did not come forward to save him. The chaplain who administered to Allen during his last days in the "condemned cell" was prepared to absolve the corporal and could not accept that he was a murderer.

One of the hill station's most sensational crimes was committed on twenty-fifth July 1927, at the height of the "season" and in the heart of the town, in Zephyr Hall, then a boarding-house. It provided a good deal of excitement for the residents of the boarding-house.

Soon after mid-day, Zephyr Hall residents were startled into brisk activity when a woman screamed and a shot rang out from one of the rooms. Other shots followed in rapid succession.

Those boarders who happened to be in the public lounge or verandah dived for the safety of their rooms; but one unhappy resident, taking the precaution of coming around a corner with his hands held well above his head, ran straight into a levelled pistol. And the man with the gun, who had just killed his wife and wounded his daughter, was still able to see some humour in the situation, for he burst into laughter! The boarder escaped unhurt. But the murderer, Mr. Owen, did not savour the situation for long. He shot himself long before the police arrived.

Ten years earlier, on twenty-fourth November 1917, another husband had shot his wife.

Mrs. Fennimore, the wife of a schoolmaster, had got herself inextricably enmeshed in a defamation law-suit, each hearing of which was more distasteful to Mr. Fennimore than the previous one. Finally he determined on his own solution. Late at night he armed himself with a loaded revolver, moved to his wife's bedside, and, finding her lying asleep on her side, shot her through the back of the head. For no accountable reason he put the weapon under her pillow, and then completed his plan. Going to the lavatory, three rooms beyond his wife's bedroom, he leaned over his loaded rifle and shot himself.

THE TOMB AND CITY OF TUGHLAQ SHAH

"Ya base Gujar
Ya rahe ujar."

(May it be inhabited by Gujars,
Or may it lie desolate.)

THE CURSE OF Saint Nizam-ud-din has been effective. The desolate, crumbling battlements of Tughlaqabad, on the outskirts of modern Delhi, look down on peaceful fields and the tent-like tomb of the warrior king who built this city. It is difficult to reconstruct the picture the city must have presented when it was built just over six centuries ago; but here and there a massive bastion less weathered by time gives one some idea of its former magnificence. Today it is a mass of ruins, the home of the jackal and the porcupine; and sometimes a leopard from the hills near Alwar takes shelter in the more inaccessible underground passageways. The only signs of human life are the temporary huts of the Gujar goatherds, lean men with sharp eyes and sun-baked limbs.

The curse which was laid on the city has been literally fulfilled.

Ghiyas-ud-din Tughlaq was one of the few rulers of the period who emerges with an almost unblemished character. The greater part of his life, up to the time he was called to the throne, was spent fighting the battles of the Khiljis, until that dynasty fell due to the follies of Kutb-ud-din Mubarak. Tughlaq was pressed to ascend the throne himself, as it was generally acknowledged that this experienced old warrior was the only man who could restore order out of the chaos then prevailing.

He was crowned in Delhi as Ghiyas-ud-din Tughlaq Shah. His father had been a Turkish slave of the Tughlaq tribe. His mother was a Jat woman, of Indian birth.

Although old in years when he came to the throne, Tughlaq was vigorous in mind and body, and his actions justified the confidence placed in him. He did not seek to conciliate a few by making enormous gifts to favoured individuals, and the only malcontents were those who were disappointed by his policy of discouraging the accumulation of great wealth. He encouraged agriculture, and land which had remained waste during the former period of misrule came again under cultivation. He superintended the collection of revenue, and ruled that the only reward of the tax-gatherer would be the exemption of his own holdings from taxation.

The rapidity with which Tughlaq made his authority felt was due partly to his excellent means of communication, by which despatches were passed on from hand to hand, either by runner or horseman. He was, in fact, the initiator of the Indian postal system. The stage for a runner was only about two-thirds of a mile (it was eight miles for the East India Company's runners), and this comparatively short distance could be covered swiftly. Huts were built along the route for the accommodation of these runners, and the system appears to have worked effectively. In the next reign, the arrival of the North African traveller Ibn Batuta at the mouth of the Indus was known in Delhi, a distance of between eight and nine hundred miles, in five days.

Tughlaq Shah abandoned Siri, the capital of his predecessors — abandoning capitals was quite fashionable at that time — and chose a new site on a barren, rocky ridge, about three miles to the east of Siri. An extensive town and citadel were raised in the short space of four years.

Today an atmosphere of melancholy grandeur broods over Tughlaqabad. In spite of the general decay, the southern face of the citadel still presents a formidable line of loopholed walls and towers. "Here," wrote the traveller Ibn Batuta, "were Tughlaq's treasures and palaces, and the great palace which he had built of gilded bricks which, when the sun rose, shone so dazzlingly that none could steadily gaze upon it." The only disadvantage was the absence of good drinking water, and this was probably one of the chief reasons why the city was later abandoned. It was for a similar reason that Akbar's great city of Fatehpur-Sikri was abandoned, and it seems strange to us today that great cities should have been built without first ascertaining the presence of a good and sufficient water supply.

The construction of Tughlaqabad had been carried out with some difficulty. There are stories of the feud that existed between Tughlaq Shah and Saint Nizam-ud-din who was at the time excavating a tank at his shrine, some five miles distant. The holy man wanted the labourers who had worked on the walls of Tughlaqabad to continue working for him at night by the light of lamps. Tughlaq, disapproving of this, prevented the sale of oil to Nizam-ud-din; but the saint, it is said, caused a light to issue from the waters of the tank, and continued with the work. Tughlaq Shah then laid a curse of bitterness upon the waters of the shrine, and the saint retaliated with the famous curse on Tughlaqabad.

Though a pious Mohammedan, Tughlaq had no intention of surrendering his authority to Nizam-ud-din. He was able to restrict the power of the saint, and this, it was said, resulted in the latter conspiring with the sultan's ambitious son Juna Khan in plotting the death of the king.

Tughlaq was away in Bengal when he received news of his son's treachery; he wrote to Nizam-ud-din saying that when he returned to his capital, Delhi would be too small to hold both of them. It was then that Nizam-ud-din made the laconic remark which has become proverbial: "*Hanuz Dihli dur ast*", "Delhi is yet far distant."

Tughlaqabad was gaily decorated to welcome the returning king. For the reception Juna Khan had erected a wooden kiosk, so flimsy that if any large animal leant against the structure, it would fall to the ground. Juna Khan then prepared a parade of elephants as part of the reception, and at a convenient moment the kiosk collapsed, burying the sultan beneath it.

The event was afterwards described in detail by Sheikh Rukhn-ud-din, who was present at the reception and who was actually warned to leave the kiosk shortly before it overturned. The arrival of spades and other implements was delayed by Juna Khan. When at length Tughlaq's body was extricated from the ruins, he was found protecting with his body his youngest and favourite son.

The tomb of Tughlaq Shah is perhaps one of the most handsome buildings outside modern Delhi; at one time it was surrounded on all sides by a small lake. There are three graves inside the tomb — those of Tughlaq Shah, his Queen, and Juna Khan himself, whose subsequent reign earned him the title of Khuni Sultan, "Bloody King". Firoz Shah, his successor, bought acquittances from all those Juna Khan had wronged, and put them in a chest at the head of his grave, that he might present them when called to judgement.

THE STORY OF KARNAL

LITTLE IS LEFT to show that the British ever had anything to do with Karnal: a decaying church tower, a forgotten cemetery, are all that remain of the unhappy cantonment that existed there from 1811 until 1841. The present town stands a little distance away, seventy-six miles from Delhi on the Grand Trunk Road.

As I drove through the sleepy town on my way to Chandigarh, I could not help noticing the church tower to the right of the road; and stopping the jeep, I walked over to investigate this forgotten monument. As I approached, the twisted iron cemetery gate clanged, and about a dozen cows and buffaloes were led out of the enclosure. The boy in charge of them gazed curiously at me. Nobody could have visited the place for years, and he must have been wondering what I was doing there.

I entered what must have been the chancel, directly beneath the bell tower. A flight of steps ran up to the belfry, but I did not trust them after all these years. I could see a patch of blue sky immediately above me. The floor was covered with cow-dung and the leavings of other animals, and I did not stay long enough to read the inscriptions on the few memorial tablets that remained on the walls.

This impression of neglect gathered force when I entered the abandoned cemetery and walked cautiously through the long grass that almost hid the graves from the path. Most of the inscriptions had worn off the stone, but as I read some of them, a small chapter of history came alive again, and the tragedy of Karnal was brought home to me.

Most of the graves belonged to women and children. Almost the entire cantonment population of Karnal had been wiped out by cholera and malarial fever when the city's drainage and the West Jumna canal met to form a swamp outside the town. Among those who perished — officers and men, their families and servants — were the wife and small daughters of Thomas Metcalfe, the Resident at Delhi. And still well-preserved is the grave of the Chaplain himself, who met the same fate as his parishioners at the age of thirty. Few people over forty are buried here. The gravestones were made in Delhi, by Hindu artisans — their names stand out small and clear at the corners of each stone — and those calamitous years must have made the undertakers rich, if they survived the epidemic themselves.

Karnal first fell into British hands in 1797, when George Thomas seized the town from the Raja of Jind. But Thomas was no "servant of the Company". He was an Irish adventurer, who owed allegiance to no one, and in the space of a few years — with great daring and skill and a few devoted followers — made himself king of all the territory between Hansi and Karnal, and beyond. He fought the French and the Marathas and, for that matter, anyone who threatened his realm, and after a few glorious years was eventually driven out of Hansi after he had rendered himself insensible from a fierce bout of drinking occasioned by the death of his best officer.

George Thomas's exploits would fill a book, but there is nothing in Karnal to remind us of his brief, blustering reign there. After his death, the town was conferred by Lord Lake upon Nawab Muhammed Khan, a Mandil Pathan.

Karnal played a small but interesting part in the suppression of the rising in Delhi in 1857. I was reminded of this when by chance I stumbled across a marble slab which marked the resting-place of General Anson, Commander-in-Chief of the British Forces in 1857. He had died at Karnal, of cholera, while on the march to Delhi.

The British force had marched all the way from Simla, a distance of about a hundred and fifty miles. The month was May, and it was impossible to march by day; the Grand Trunk Road was then an endless ribbon of burning sand.

Years later, an officer, recalling the march, wrote:

"The stars were bright in the dark deep sky and the fireflies flashed from bush to bush.

"Along the road came the heavy roll of the guns, mixed with the jangling of bits and the clanking of the steel scabbards of the cavalry; the infantry marched behind with a deep, dull tread; camels and bullock-carts, with innumerable camp servants, toiled along for miles in the rear; while gigantic elephants stalked over bush and stone by the side of the road."

Elephants were used to pull the heavy guns.

But Karnal made history long before the British came to

India. It is said to have been founded by Raja Karna, champion of the Kauravas, in the great war of the *Mahabharata*. It is the place where the Persian invader Nadir Shah defeated the Moghul Emperor Muhammed Shah in 1739. The battle lasted two hours, and 20,000 of the Emperor's soldiers were killed. The next day Nadir Shah marched to Delhi, to sack the city and massacre its inhabitants.

No one passing through Karnal today would easily connect it with the momentous events it has seen. It is just like any other district town, its only relics a crumbling city wall and a neglected cemetery.

Should anyone be deterred from spending too much time in Karnal by my account of the epidemic that once wiped out its cantonment, I ought to mention here that the canal was re-aligned in 1875, and Karnal is today as healthy as any town in the Punjab or Hariana.

AN ENGLISH JESTER AT THE MOGHUL COURT

IN THE DIARIES and correspondence of Sir Thomas Roe, the English Ambassador to the Court of Jehangir, there are frequent references to a number of Englishmen who, for a few colourful years, strutted about the Indian scene, and then were heard of no more. The strangest of this group of fortune-hunters and eccentrics was Thomas Corryat, known at home as the "Odcombe legstretcher", a man of many parts who had earned a certain literary reputation as the author of *Corryat's Crudities*, a whimsical book on continental travel.

Corryat, the son of a Somerset clergyman, gained early distinction as a sort of buffoon at the court of James I. His physical peculiarities — a peaked "sugar-loaf formation of head" perched on an ungainly frame — added to a ready wit, made him a favourite with the English king who later came to be called "the wisest fool in Christendom". Encouraged by his sovereign, he began, in 1608, a long series of wanderings which took him into almost every corner of Europe and resulted in his travel book, the *Crudities*, which was published by patrons whose help he obtained by "unwearied pertinacity and unblushing opportunity". The volume was foreworded with some mock-heroic verses by Ben Jonson, but the ridicule was lost on Tom Corryat, whose sense of humour lacked subtlety, thus rendering him immune to the barbs of satire.

In 1612 Corryat again started on his travels, this time in the direction of the East. He tramped through the Holy Land, on to Nineveh and Babylon, down the Euphrates valley to Baghdad, through Persia to Kandahar, and down into India. He turned up at Agra in 1615, and presented himself before Ambassador Roe, who had known the wanderer at King James's court. Sir Thomas was by no means pleased to see Corryat, who was far from being the ideal image of the Englishman which Roe wished to project for the benefit of Jehangir; but he felt it was his duty to help the traveller before speeding him on his way.

Tom Corryat, however, was in no hurry to move on. He

boasted that he had made his way through Asia on little more than two pence a day, having in fact lived off the generosity of various benefactors. At Agra, the Moghul capital, he soon made himself at home. A natural linguist, he acquired such proficiency in Hindustani that it was said of him that, in a quarrel with the Ambassador's troublesome washerwoman, he reduced the lady to silence within an hour. . . .

He made more dangerous use of his knowledge of the language one evening at the time of Mohammedan prayer when, in response to the muezzin's cry, "There is no God but Allah, and Mohammed is his prophet", he shouted in Hindustani that the true prophet was Christ. It says a great deal for the tolerance which then prevailed at the Moghul capital that this insult was overlooked as the indiscretion of the half-witted "English fakir". Corryat, however, made up for this blunder when, having somehow managed to obtain an audience of Jehangir, he recited a flattering eulogy of the Emperor, in Persian. Jehangir was both amused and pleased by this barefaced flattery, and dismissed Corryat with some kind words and a gift of a hundred rupees.

When Sir Thomas Roe heard of the goings-on of his itinerant guest, he was furious, and raved at Corryat for an hour, accusing him of degrading the good name of England.

"But," said Corryat, in describing the encounter, "I answered our ambassador in such a stout and resolute manner that he ceased nibbling at me."

A time came when Tom Corryat, having exhausted the financial possibilities of the Moghul capital, decided to return home. Roe, only too happy to be rid of so embarrassing a guest, gave him a letter of introduction to the English consul at Alleppo, requesting the consul to receive Corryat with courtesy, "for you shall find him a very honest poor wretch", and asking him to pay the bearer £10. Corryat was hurt by the expression "honest poor wretch", but he accepted the letter.

Leaving Agra, Corryat made for Surat, where he was hospitably received by the members of the English factory. In the course of a conversation mention was made of a shipment of sack which had just arrived from England. The wanderer's eyes glistened at this mention of his favourite drink, which he had long been without.

"Sack! Sack!" he exclaimed. "Is there any such thing as sack? I pray you, give me some sack!" The factors obliged him, and

Corryat, drinking to excess, collapsed dramatically. A few days later he was dead.

Tom Corryat was laid to rest near Surat. Time has obliterated all traces of his grave; but local tradition has identified it with a monument in the Muslim style at Rajgari, a village near Swally, the old seaport of Surat. The memory of this strange individual's eruption into seventeenth-century India will always fascinate those who follow the lesser-known paths of history.

GEMS FROM A BYGONE AGE

THE ADVERTISEMENTS of a bygone era are often a livelier guide to the social life of a period than any number of serious tomes. During recent rummagings in a junkshop, I discovered a copy of *The Calcutta Magazine* of May 1882, still surviving on paper that was brown and delicate with age. It was not the rather pompous literary contents of the magazine that attracted me but the diversity of its advertisements. These were probably common enough eighty-five years ago. Read today, they provide vivid glimpses into the past, into the fashions, literary tastes, and medical remedies indulged in by our grandparents.

I have made a small selection of those advertisements most likely to interest and amuse the modern reader, and reproduce them here without any changes.

MESSRS. PISTI & PELEKANOS
104, Clive Street,

Are now in a position to offer their customers and friends genuine Egyptian Cigarettes and choice Turkey Tobacco, fresh consignments of which are received every fortnight.

Also Manilla, Burma, and Trichinopoly Cigars, of the best qualities, various Meerschaum Pipes, Cigar and Cigarette Holders, Russian Caviare, Italian Macaroni, Pure Ground Coffee, and finest Bath and Toilet Sponges.

The following are some testimonials for Darlington's Pain-Curer:

Baboo Kunny Lal of Jumna Pershad & Co., Bankers of Muzufferpore, writes: — "Please send me another dozen small bottles of Darlington's Pain-Curer. I have used it on the ringworm, and pains on the back, and it has cured them."

Mr. Geo. Kiernander, Inspector of Customs, Calcutta, writes:

— "Kindly send me a large-sized bottle of Darlington's Pain-Curer. I find its effects wonderful in relieving troublesome coughs."

His Highness Raja Pratab Sah of Tehri Garhwal State, N.W. Provinces, writes: — "It affords me much pleasure in informing you that the two bottles of Darlington's Pain-Curer which I took from you has given me an extraordinary relief from the rheumatism I have been suffering since last 6 months. Therefore I request you to send me 2 bottles more (large size) as I wish to take this valuable medicine with me on my tour towards the Himalaya mountains."

THE "SOUTH INDIAN POST"
Published Weekly.
Rates of Subscription,
One Rupee per Mensem.
ADVERTISING RATES,
One anna per line for each insertion.

SCOTCH WHISKEY
"BENVORLICH WHISKEY"
As supplied to the Houses of Parliament.
Without doubt the finest ever imported into India,
Rs. 24 per case.

AMERICAN KEROSENE OIL
Devoe's Imperial Brilliant,
Per case of two — (10 gallons) Rs. 4-8-0
Special rates for 10 cases and upwards.

SIMPLE, SAFE AND CERTAIN: HOLLOWAY'S OINTMENT

Is a certain remedy for bad legs, bad breasts, and ulcerations of all kinds. It acts miraculously in healing ulcerations, curing skin diseases, and in arresting and subduing all inflammations.

MR. J. T. COOPER,

in his account of his extraordinary travels in China, published in 1871, says, "I had with me a quantity of Holloway's Ointment. I gave some to the people, and nothing could exceed their gratitude; and, in consequence, milk, fowls, butter, and horse-feed poured in upon us, until at last a teaspoonful of ointment was worth a fowl and any quantity of peas, and the demand became so great that I was obliged to lock up the remaining stock."

Sold throughout the Civilized World.
Moderately priced.

HORSES.
A. MILTON & CO.
Have on hand for Commission Sale a large number of
WALERS ! WALERS ! WALERS !
Imported ex Ship *Rialto* and *Argus* by the well-known Shipper, MR. WM. MACKLIN.
The Ship "Cingalese" has arrived with a shipment of 170 horses and a number of Racing Ponies, specially selected for the Calcutta Market. They are now arranged for inspection at our Horse Mart.
CRUSHED FOOD.
For Horses at Rs. 2-2 per maund.
For Cattle at Rs. 1-10 per maund.
Exclusive of Bags.
Every attention paid to Sick Horses.

THE AKHBAR-I-SOUDAGUR, SUMACHARDURPUN & BOMBAYCHABOOK OR
The Native Merchants' Daily Gazette.
The First and the Most Widely Circulated Goojrathee Daily Paper in Bombay

---

DR KING'S DANDELION and QUININE
Liver Pills (without Mercury).

The Best Remedy for Biliousness, Stomach Derangement, Flatulence, Pains Between the Shoulders, Bad Appetite, Indigestion, Acidity, Head-Ache, Heart Burn, and all other symptoms of disordered liver and dyspepsia.

INFALLIBLE, SUCCESSFUL and SURE CURE
For CHOLERA

Parties are requested to inform MRS. LUCAS, at 254 and 255, Bow-Bazar Street, without delay and loss of time. Charges according to the circumstances of patients.

Mrs. Lucas begs to state that no surgical operations will be performed but simply a few drops of her most valuable medicine will be administered.

GLORIES OF THE HOOKAH

"THE MUSIC OF ITS SOUND puts the warbling of the nightingale to shame, and the fragrance of its perfume brings a blush to the cheek of the rose."

It was with these words that a Persian poet went into rhapsodies over the hookah, the smoking of which had become fashionable with the nobles of Akbar's court shortly after tobacco, "the fragrant weed," had been introduced into India. Akbar himself did not smoke; but hookah-smoking was considered a cool and wholesome habit, and when the Persian fashion took India by storm, Maharajas and Nawabs found in the hookah a new object of luxury, and one capable of endless decoration. They opened up a new field for artistic talent. Silver State Hookahs were of considerable height, running to three feet, with coils of tubing which terminated in a silver mouthpiece. Some of copper gilt, with a very rich deep blue and enamel, were works of great beauty. The "Chillum", or upper bowl which contained the tobacco, was itself a work of art.

There have been many variants of the hookah, from Sind to Tanjore, and a South Indian variant is the "Narghile", which has a bowl made of a real coconut, usually mounted in silver.

The "hubble-bubble" — as the hookah was sometimes called by Europeans — became very popular with Englishmen who came out to India during the second half of the eighteenth century. This was a period when Englishmen readily took to Indian customs and pastimes, a happy attitude that was to disappear with the advent, in the following century, of Victorian prudery and Christian evangelicism. After 1857, few Englishmen smoked hookhas. But in Warren Hastings' time, the hookah was a respectable household article in both Indian and European households. When Mrs. Hastings was sending out invitations to a concert, she begged that no servants be brought, with the sole exception of "hukka-bardars" — men responsible for the upkeep and maintenance of their masters' hookahs.

"It is chiefly in Bengal", wrote de Grandpre in 1789, "when

smoking after meals is customary that the hukka is in use. Every hukka-bardar prepares separately that of his master in an adjoining apartment, and entering together with the dessert, they range around the table. It is scarcely possible to see through the clouds of smoke which fill the apartment. The rage of smoking extends even to the ladies, and the highest compliment they can pay a man is to give him preference by smoking his hukka. In this case it is a point of politeness to take off the mouthpiece he is using and substitute a fresh one; which he presents to the lady with his hukka, who soon returns it."

The hukka-bardar's chief duty was to have the hookah ready whenever his master wanted it. His duties were not as light, as they might seem. The "snake" of the hookah — a flexible tube some fifteen feet long — had to be kept clean. Mixing the tobacco with cinnamon and molasses, and adding musk or rose-water to the bowl, were time-consuming duties. In order that the smoke might pass easily through the "snake", this had to be kept moist. And to prevent the clothes of the smoker from getting wet, it was usual to wrap a cloth round the part of the pipe near the mouthpiece.

Some smokers expected their hukka-bardars to make all the necessary purchases of tobacco, spices, molasses, fireballs, chillums and pipes. The best tobacco was reputed to come from Bilsa in the Bombay area, but only a small portion of it, was used in the mix. The average hukka-bardar used to make something for himself out of supplying tobacco. More 'Bilsa tobacco' was sold than was ever grown!

When the hukka-bardar brought the hookah to his master, he usually brought along with it a small carpet of some pleasing design. The pleasures of smoking were enhanced by a back-

When the Persian fashion took India by storm, Maharajahs and Nawabs found in hookahs a new object of luxury and one capable of intricate decoration. It opened up a new field for artistic talent. These silver State Hookahs were of considerable height, running to three feet, with coils of tubing which terminate in a silver mouth-piece. The one in the illustration is 30 inches high. Some, of copper gilt with a very rich deep blue and green enamel, were works of great beauty. The "Chillum", or upper bowl which contained the tobacco, was itself a work of art. (See opposite page).

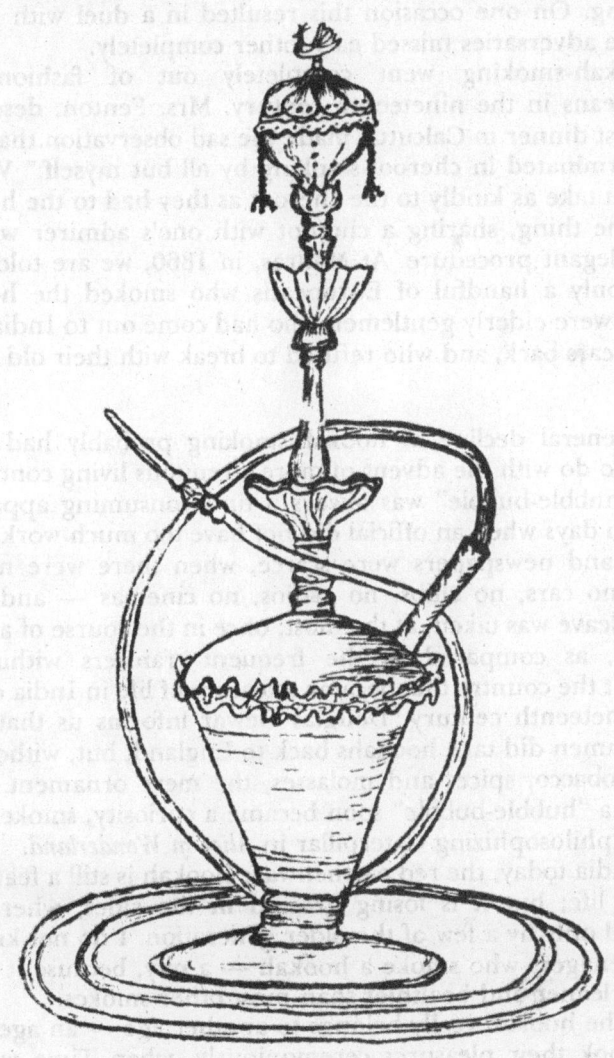

Great Indian Hookah

ground of soothing colour and design. It was considered a grave offence to step over someone else's hookah-carpet while he was smoking. On one occasion this resulted in a duel with pistols, but the adversaries missed each other completely.

Hookah-smoking went completely out of fashion with Europeans in the nineteenth century. Mrs. Fenton, describing her first dinner in Calcutta, made the sad observation that "dinner terminated in cheroot-smoking by all but myself." Women did not take as kindly to the cheroot as they had to the hookah. For one thing, sharing a cheroot with one's admirer wasn't a very elegant procedure. At Madras, in 1860, we are told there were only a handful of Europeans who smoked the hookah. These were elderly gentlemen who had come out to India some forty years back, and who refused to break with their old habits.

The general decline of hookah-smoking probably had something to do with the advent of more strenuous living conditions. The "hubble-bubble" was always a time-consuming apparatus: ideal in days when an official did not have too much work, when books and newspapers were scarce, when there were no railways, no cars, no clubs, no radios, no cinemas — and when home-leave was taken, at the most, once in the course of a man's service, as compared to the frequent transfers within and without the country that became a feature of life in India during the nineteenth century. Douglas Dewar informs us that some Englishmen did take hookahs back to England; but, without the right tobacco, spices and molasses, the mere ornament in the home, a "hubble-bubble" soon became a curiosity, smoked only by the philosophizing Caterpillar in *Alice in Wonderland*.

In India today, the red earthenware hookah is still a feature of village life; but it is losing ground in the cities, where it is smoked only by a few of the older generation. I do not know of any teenagers who smoke a hookah — a pity, because it is certainly cleaner and healthier than most other smokes.

But the hookah really belongs to another age — an age when men took their pleasures ceremoniously, when Time was not worshipped, and when the minutes were, somehow, slower in passing than they are today.

GRANDFATHER'S EARTHQUAKE

"IF EVER THERE'S A CALAMITY," Grandmother used to say, "it will find Grandfather in his bath." Grandfather loved his bath — which he took in a large round aluminium tub — and sometimes spent as long as an hour in it, 'wallowing' as he called it, and splashing around like a boy.

He was in his bath during the earthquake that convulsed Bengal and Assam on 12 June 1897 — an earthquake so severe that even today the region of the great Brahmaputra river basin hasn't settled down. Not long ago it was reported that the entire Shillong plateau had moved an appreciable distance away from the Brahmaputra towards the Bay of Bengal. According to the Geological Survey of India, this shift has been taking place gradually over the past eighty years.

Had Grandfather been alive, he would have added one more clipping to his scrapbook on the earthquake. The clipping goes in anyway, because the scrapbook is now with his children. More than newspaper accounts of the disaster, it was Grandfather's own letters and memoirs that made the earthquake seem recent and vivid; for he, along with Grandmother and two of their children (one of them my father), was living in Shillong, a picturesque little hill station in Assam, when the earth shook and the mountains heaved.

As I have mentioned, Grandfather was in his bath, splashing about, and did not hear the first rumbling. But Grandmother was in the garden, hanging out or taking in the washing (she could never remember which) when, suddenly, the animals began making a hideous noise — a sure intimation of a natural disaster, for animals sense the approach of an earthquake much more quickly than humans.

The crows all took wing, wheeling wildly overhead and cawing loudly. The chickens flapped in circles, as if they were being chased. Two dogs sitting on the verandah suddenly jumped up and ran out with their tails between their legs. Within half a minute of her noticing the noise made by the animals, Grandmother heard a rattling, rumbling noise, like the approach of a train.

The noise increased for about a minute, and then there was the first trembling of the ground. The animals by this time all seemed to have gone mad. Treetops lashed backwards and forwards, doors banged and windows shook, and Grandmother swore later that the house actually swayed in front of her. She had difficulty in standing straight, though this could have been due more to the trembling of her knees than to the trembling of the ground.

The first shock lasted for about a minute and a half. "I was in my tub having a bath," Grandfather wrote for posterity, "which for the first time in the last two months I had taken in the afternoon instead of in the morning. My wife and children and the ayah were downstairs. Then the shock came, accompanied by a loud rumbling sound under the earth and a quaking which increased in intensity every second. It was like putting so many shells in a basket, and shaking them up with a rapid sifting motion from side to side.

"At first I did not realize what it was that caused my tub to sway about and the water to splash. I rose up, and found the earth heaving, while the wash-stand, basin, ewer, cups and glasses danced and rocked about in the most hideous fashion. I rushed to the inner door to open it and search for wife and children, but could not move the dratted door as boxes, furniture and plaster had come up against it. The back door was the only way of escape. I managed to burst it open, and, thank God, was able to get out. Sections of the thatched roof had slithered down on the four sides like a pack of cards and blocked all the exits and entrances.

"With only a towel wrapped around my waist, I ran out into the open to the front of the house, but found only my wife there. The whole front of the house was blocked by the fallen section of thatch from the roof. Through this I broke my way under the iron railings and extricated the others. The bearer had pluckily borne the weight of the whole thatched roof section on his back as it had slithered down, and in this way saved the ayah and children from being crushed beneath it."

After the main shock of the earthquake had passed, minor shocks took place at regular intervals of five minutes or so, all through the night. But during that first shake-up the town of Shillong was reduced to ruin and rubble. Everything made of masonry was brought to the ground. Government House, the post office, the jail, all tumbled down. When the jail fell, the prisoners, instead of making their escape, sat huddled on the road waiting for the Superintendent to come to their aid.

"The ground began to heave and shake," wrote a young girl in a newspaper called *The Englishman*. "I stayed on my bicycle for a second, and then fell off and got up and tried to run, staggering about from side to side of the road. To my left I saw great clouds of dust, which I afterwards discovered to be houses falling and the earth slipping from the sides of the hills. To my right I saw the small dam at the end of the lake torn asunder and the water rushing out, the wooden bridge across the lake break in two and the sides of the lake falling in; and at my feet the ground cracking and opening. I was wild with fear and didn't know which way to turn."

The lake rose up like a mountain, and then totally disappeared, leaving only a swamp of red mud. Not a house was left standing. People were rushing about, wives looking for husbands, parents looking for children, not knowing whether their loved ones were alive or dead. A crowd of people had collected on the cricket ground, which was considered the safest place; but Grandfather and the family took shelter in a small shop on the road outside his house. The shop was a rickety wooden structure, which had always looked as though it would fall down in a strong wind. But it withstood the earthquake.

And then the rain came and it poured. This was extraordinary, because before the earthquake there wasn't a cloud to be seen; but, five minutes after the shock, Shillong was enveloped in cloud and mist. The shock was felt for more than a hundred miles on the Assam-Bengal Railway. A train was overturned at Shamshernagar; another was derailed at Mantolla. Over a thousand people lost their lives in the Cherrapunji Hills, and in other areas, too, the death roll was heavy.

The Brahmaputra burst its banks and many cultivators were drowned in the flood. A tiger was found drowned. And in North Bhagalpur, where the earthquake started, two elephants sat down in the bazaar and refused to get up until the following morning.

Over a hundred men who were at work in Shillong's Government printing press were caught in the building when it collapsed, and, though the men of a Gurkha regiment did splendid rescue work, only a few were brought out alive. One of those killed in Shillong was Mr McCabe, a British official. Grandfather described the ruins of Mr McCabe's house: "Here a bedpost, there a sword, a broken desk or chair, a bit of torn carpet, a well-known hat with its Indian Civil Service colours, battered books, all speaking reminiscences of the man we mourn."

While most houses collapsed where they stood, Government House, it seems, 'fell backwards'. The church was a mass of red stones in ugly disorder. The organ was a tortured wreck.

A few days later the family, with other refugees, were making their way to Calcutta to stay with friends or relatives. It was a slow, tedious journey, with many interruptions, for the roads and railway lines had been badly damaged and passengers had often to be transported in trolleys. Grandfather was rather struck at the stoicism displayed by an assistant engineer. At one station a telegram was handed to the engineer informing him that his bungalow had been destroyed. "Beastly nuisance," he observed with an aggrieved air. "I've seen it cave in during a storm, but this is the first time it has played me such a trick on account of an earthquake."

The family got to Calcutta to find the inhabitants of the capital in a panic; for they too had felt the quake and were expecting it to recur. The damage in Calcutta was slight compared to the devastation elsewhere, but nerves were on edge, and people slept in the open or in carriages. Cracks and fissures had appeared in a number of old buildings, and Grandfather was among the many who were worried at the proposal to fire a salute of sixty guns on Jubilee Day (the Diamond Jubilee of Queen Victoria); they felt the gunfire would bring down a number of shaky buildings. Obviously Grandfather did not wish to be caught in his bath a second time. However, Queen Victoria was not to be deprived of her salute. The guns were duly fired, and Calcutta remained standing.

KIPLING'S SIMLA

EVERY MARCH, when the rhododendrons stain the slopes crimson with their blooms, a sturdy little steam engine goes huffing and puffing through the 103 tunnels between Kalka and Simla.

This is probably the most picturesque and romantic way of approaching the hill station although the journey by road is much quicker. But quite recently I went to Simla by a little-used route, the road from Dehra Dun via Nahan and Solan, it takes one first through the sub-tropical Siwaliks, and then after Nahan into the foothills and some beautiful and extensive pine forests, before joining the main highway near Solan. By bus it is a tedious ten-hour journey, but by car it is a picturesque ride, and there is very little traffic to contend with. . . .

But those train journeys stand out in the memory — the little restaurant at Barog, just before the train reaches Dharampur, where the roads for Sanawar and Kasauli branch off; and the gorge at Tara Devi, opening out to give the weary traveller the splendid and uplifting panorama of the city of Simla straddling the side of the mountain.

In Rudyard Kipling's time (that is, in the 1870s and 80s), travellers spent the night at Kalka and then covered the 60-odd hill miles by tonga, a rugged and exhausting journey. It was especially hard on invalids who had travelled long distances to recuperate in the cool clear air of the mountains.

In his story "The Other Man" (*Plain Tales From the Hills; 1890*), Kipling describes the unhappy results of the tonga-ride on one such visitor:

"Sitting on the back seat, very square and firm, with one hand on the awning stanchion and the wet pouring off his hat and moustache, was the Other Man — dead. The sixty-mile uphill jolt had been too much for his valve, I suppose. The tonga-driver said, 'This Sahib died two stages out of Solan. Therefore, I tied him with a rope, lest he should fall out by the way, and so we came to Simla. Will the Sahib give me *bakshish?* "It', pointing to the Other Man, 'should have given one rupee'."

Today's visitor to Simla need have no qualms about the journey by road, which is swift and painless (provided you drive carefully), but the coolies at the Simla bus-stand will be found to be as adamant as Kipling's tonga-driver in claiming their *bakshish*.

Simla is worth a visit at any time of the year, even during the monsoon. The monsoon season is one of the most beautiful times of the year in the Himalayas, with the mist trailing up the valleys, and the hill slopes, a lush green, thick with ferns and wild flowers. The call of the *kastura*, or whistling-thrush, can be heard in every glen, while the barbet cries insistently from the tree tops.

Not far from Christ Church is the corner where a great fictional character, Lurgan Sahib, had his shop — Lurgan being the curio-dealer who took the young Kim in hand and trained him as a spy. He was based on a real-life character, who had his shop here. Kipling wrote *Kim* a few years after he had left India. His nostalgia for India, and in particular for the hills, come through in his description of Kim's arrival in Simla in the company of the Afghan horse-dealer, Mahbub Ali.

" 'A fair land — a most beautiful land is this of Hind — and the land of the Five Rivers is fairer than all,' Kim half-chanted. 'Into it I will go again. . . . Once gone, who shall find me? Look, Hajji, is yonder the city of Simla? Allah! What a city!' "

They lead their horses below the main road into the lower Simla bazaar — "the crowded rabbit-warren that climbs up from the valley to the Town Hall at an angle of forty-five!" And then together they set off "through the mysterious dusk, full of the noises of a city below the hillside and the breath of a cool wind in deodar-crowned Jakko, shouldering the stars."

Shouldering the stars! That is how I always think of Simla — standing on the Ridge and looking up through the clear air into the vault of the heavens, where the stars seem so much nearer. . . . And they are reflected below, in the myriad lights of the shops and houses.

For those who want a bit of history, Simla came into being at the end of the Anglo-Gurkha War (1814-16), when most of the surrounding district — captured by the Gurkhas during their invasion — was restored to various States; but the land on which Simla stands was retained by the British — "for services rendered!" Lieutenant Rose built the first house, a thatched wooden cottage, in 1819. His successor, Lieutenant Kennedy, in 1822 built a permanent house, which survived until it was destroyed in a fire a couple of years ago. In 1827 Lord Amherst spent several months at Kennedy House and from then on Simla grew in favour with the British. Its early history can be read in more detail in Sir Edward Buck's *Simla Past and Present*, copies of which sometimes turn up in secondhand bookshops.

From 1865 until the Second World War, Simla was the summer capital of the Government of India. Later it served as the capital of East Punjab pending the construction of Chandigarh, and today of course it is the capital of Himachal Pradesh.

It is not, however, as a capital city that Simla attracts the visitor but as a place of lovely winding walks, magnificent views, and romantic links with the past. Compared with some of our hillstations, it is well looked after; the streets are clean and uncluttered, the old Georgian-style buildings still stand. And the trees are more in evidence than at other hill resorts.

Simla has a special place in my affections. It was there that I went to school, and it was there that my father and I spent our happiest times together.

We stayed on Elysium Hill; took long walks to Kasumpti and around Jakko Hill; sipped milk-shakes at Davico's; saw plays at the Gaiety Theatre (happily still in existence); fed the monkeys at the temple on Jakko; picnicked in Chota Simla. All this during the short summer break when my father (on leave from the Air Force) came up to see me. He told me stories of phantom-rickshaws and enchanted forests and planted in me the seeds of my writing career. I was only ten when he died. But he had already passed on to me his love for the hills. And even after I had finished school and grown to manhood, I was to return to the hills again and again — to Simla and Mussoorie, Himachal and Garhwal — because once the mountains are in your blood, there is no escape.

Simla beckons. I must return. And, like Kim, I will take the last bend near Summer Hill and look up and exclaim: "Ah! What a city!"

"Romance brought up the nine-fifteen," wrote Kipling and there is still romance to be found on trains and at lonely stations. Small wayside stations have always fascinated me. Manned sometimes by just one or two men, and often situated in the middle of a damp sub-tropical forest, or clinging to the mountainside on the way to Simla or Darjeeling these little stations are, for me, outposts of romance, lonely symbols of the spirit that led a certain kind of pioneer to lay tracks into the remote corners of the earth.

Recently I was at such a wayside stop, on a line that went through the Terai forests near the foothills of the Himalayas. At about ten at night, the *khilasi*, or station watchman, lit his kerosene lamp and started walking up the track into the jungle. He was a Gujar, and his true vocation was the keeping of buffaloes, but the breaking up of his tribe had led him into this strange new occupation.

"Where are you going?" I asked.

"To see if the tunnel is clear," he said. "The Mail train comes in twenty minutes."

So I went with him, a furlong or two along the tracks, through a deep cutting which led to the tunnel. Every night, the *khilasi* walked through the dark tunnel, and then stood outside to wave his lamp to the oncoming train as a signal that the track was clear. If the engine driver did not see the lamp, he stopped the train. It always slowed down near the cutting.

Having inspected the tunnel, we stood outside, waiting for the train. It seemed a long time coming. There was no moon, and the dense forest seemed to be trying to crowd us into the narrow cutting. The sounds of the forest came to us on the night wind — the belling of a *sambhar*, the cry of a fox, told us that perhaps a tiger or a leopard was on the prowl. There were strange nocturnal bird and insect sounds; and then silence.

The *khilasi* stood outside the tunnel, trimming his lamp, listening to the faint sounds of the jungle — sounds which only he, a Gujar who had grown up on the fringe of the forest, could identify and understand. Something made him stand very still for a few moments, peering into the darkness, and I could sense that everything was not as it should be.

"There is something in the tunnel," he said.

I could hear nothing at first; but then there came a regular sawing sound, just like the sound of someone sawing through the branch of a tree.

"*Baghera!*" whispered the *khilasi*. He had said enough to enable me to recognise the sound — that of a leopard trying to find its mate.

I thought how fortunate we were that it had not been there when we walked through the tunnel. A leopard is unpredictable. But so is a *khilasi*.

"The train will be coming soon," he whispered urgently. "We must drive the animal out of the tunnel, or it will be killed."

He must have sensed my astonishment, because he said, "Do not worry, Sahib. I know this leopard well. We have seen each other many times. He has a weakness for stray dogs and goats, but he will not harm us."

He gave me his small hand-axe to hold, and, raising his lamp high, started walking into the tunnel, shouting at the top of his voice to try and scare away the animal. I followed close behind him.

We had gone about twenty yards into the tunnel when the light from the *khilasi's* lamp fell on the leopard, who was crouching between the tracks, only about fifteen feet from us.

He was not a big leopard, but he was lithe and sinewy. Baring his teeth in a snarl, he went down on his belly, tail twitching, and I felt sure he was going to spring.

The *khilasi* and I both shouted together. Our voices rang and echoed through the tunnel. And the frightened leopard, uncertain of how many human beings were in there with him, turned swiftly and disappeared into the darkness.

As we returned to the tunnel entrance, the rails began to hum and we knew the train was coming.

I put my hand to one of the rails and felt its tremor. And then the engine came round the bend, hissing at us, scattering sparks into the darkness, defying the jungle as it roared through the steep sides of the cutting. It charged straight at the tunnel, and into it, thundering past us like some beautiful dragon from my childhood dreams. And when it had gone the silence returned, and the forest breathed again. Only the rails still trembled with the passing of the train.

As they tremble now to the passing of my own train, rushing through the night with its complement of precious humans, while somewhere at a lonely cutting in the foothills, a small thin man, who must always remain a firefly to these travelling thousands, lights up the darkness for steam engines and panthers.

And yet, for the *khilasi* himself, the incident I have recalled was not an adventure; it was a duty, a job of work, an everyday incident.

For me, all are significant: the lighted compartment, with its farmers, shopkeepers, artisans, clerks and occasional pick-pockets; and the lonely wayside stop, with its uncorrupted lamplighter

Romance still rides the nine-fifteen.

BIBLIOGRAPHY

BODYCOT, F. (Compiler). *Guide to Mussoorie.* (Mafasilite Press, Mussoorie, 1907)

COMPTON, HERBERT. (Compiler). *A Particular Account of the European Military Adventurers of Hindustan.* (Fisher Unwin, London, 1892)

DEWAR, DOUGLAS. *In the Days of the Company.* (Thacker Spink, Calcutta, 1920)

EDWARDES, MICHAEL. *The Orchid House.* (Cassell, London, 1960)

FANSHAWE, H.C. *Delhi Past and Present.* (John Murray, London, 1902)

FAY. *Mrs. Fay's Letters from India.* (Calcutta, 1908)

FORREST, SIR GEORGE. *Cities of India.* (Constable, London, 1903)

FRANKLIN, COLONEL WILLIAM. *The Military Memoirs of George Thomas.* (Calcutta, 1803)

FRASER, J. BAILLIE. *The Military Memoirs of James Skinner.* (London, 1851)

FRENCH, C.J. *A Tour of Upper India.* (Printed by the author, Simla, 1872)

GREY, C. and GARRETT, H.L.O. *European Adventurers of Northern India.* (Keeper of the Punjab Records) (Lahore, 1929)

HEBER, REGINALD. *A Journey Through the Upper Provinces of India.* 2 vols. (Murray, London, 1828)

KEENE, H.G. *Hindustan under the Free Lances* (Brown Langham, London, 1907)

KEENE, H.G. *Madhava Rao Sindhia.* (Oxford University Press, 1891)

KEENE, H.G. *The Great Anarchy.* (Thacker, Calcutta, 1901)

MAFASILITE PRESS, Mussoorie: *A Mussoorie Miscellany.* (1936)

MAZUMDAR, K.C. *Imperial Agra of the Moghuls.* (Agra, 1946)

OATEN, E.F. *European Travellers in India, 1400-1700.* (London, 1909)

PARKES, LADY FANNY. *Diary of the Wanderings of a Pilgrim in Search of the Picturesque.* 2 vols. (London, 1850)

PEARSE, COL. HUGH. *The Hearseys : Five Generations of an Anglo-Indian Family.* (Blackwood, London & Edinburgh, 1905)

SEN, S. N. *Delhi and Its Monuments.* (A. Mukherjee, Calcutta, 1948)

SHARP, SIR HENRY. *Delhi, Its Story and Buildings.* (Oxford University Press, 1921)

SLEEMAN, W.H. *Rambles and Recollections of an Indian Official.* 2 vols. (Hatchard, London, 1844)

SMITH, LEWIS FERDINAND. *A Sketch of the Regular Corps in the Service of the Native Princes of India.* (Calcutta, 1805)

TOD, LT.COLONEL, JAMES. *Annals of Rajasthan.* (Smith, Elder, London, 1829)

TWINING, THOMAS. *Travels in India a Hundred Years Ago.* (London, 1893)

WRIGHT, ARNOLD, *Early English Adventurers in India.* (London, 1917)

YOUNG, DESMOND. *Fountain of the Elephants.* (Collins, London, 1959)